PURPLE HEART

PURPLE HEART

BY PATRICIA McCORMICK

Balzer + Bray
An Imprint of HarperCollins*Publishers*

Balzer + Bray is an imprint of HarperCollins Publishers.

Library of Congress Cataloging-in-Publication Data
McCormick, Patricia, date
    Purple Heart / by Patricia McCormick. — 1st ed.
        p.   cm.
    Summary: While recuperating in a Baghdad hospital from a traumatic brain
injury sustained during the Iraq War, eighteen-year-old soldier Matt Duffy
struggles to recall what happened to him and how it relates to his ten-year-old
friend Ali.
    ISBN 978-0-06-173090-0 (trade bdg.) — ISBN 978-0-06-173091-7 (lib.
bdg.)
    1. Iraq War, 2003– —Juvenile fiction. [1. Iraq War, 2003– —Fiction.
2. Soldiers—Fiction. 3. Brain damage—Fiction. 4. Hospitals—Fiction.
5. Memory—Fiction. 6. Street children—Fiction.] I. Title.
PZ7.M13679Pur 2009   2009001757
[Fic]—dc22   CIP
                                                                             AC

Typography by Carla Weise
09 10 11 12 13   CG/RRDB   10 9 8 7 6 5 4 3 2 1
❖
First Edition

For Brandon

In Memoriam:

Army Sergeant Sherwood Baker

Army Specialist Joshua Justice Henry

Marine Lance Corporal Patrick B. Kenny

Army First Lieutenant Neil Anthony Santoriello

Marine Lance Corporal William Brett Wightman

"CAN YOU FEEL THAT, PRIVATE?"

Matt Duffy awoke to a tingling sensation in his foot. He lifted his head and took in the sight of a man in green scrubs standing at the end of his bed. The sensation in his foot, it seemed, had something to do with the man.

Matt closed his eyes, let his head fall back on the pillow—and felt a terrible throbbing at the base of his skull.

The tingling in his foot grew stronger, annoying, a series of pinpricks. Matt opened his eyes, looked past the man in scrubs, and saw that he was in a long, narrow room with two rows of metal beds. Across from him, a soldier in a gray T-shirt and shorts sat on the edge of the mattress. The soldier, a baby-faced kid with red hair and freckles, seemed to be staring at something in his lap.

1

Matt squinted. The kid wasn't holding anything at all, it turned out; he was looking at his right arm, at a tight, flesh-colored bandage that ended in a stump where his hand should have been.

Another, sharper jab at his foot. "Private Duffy," said the man at the end of the bed. The man had dark, almond-shaped eyes and was wearing a Hawaiian-print surgical cap. He was, apparently, probing the sole of Matt's foot with something sharp. "Can you feel that?"

A voice, thick and slow, said something that sounded like "Yeeeaaugh." It was, Matt realized, his voice.

Another pinprick. This time on his leg. "And that?"

Matt nodded.

"Can you wiggle your toes?"

Matt looked down toward the foot of the bed. The feet sticking out from the green army blanket were pale and almost delicate, not like his at all. He bit his lip and concentrated. The toes moved.

"Good." The man came around from the foot of the bed to the side. "Now your fingers."

His fingers also cooperated while Matt watched, as if from far away.

"Your legs?"

It took all his strength, but he was able to raise them, one at a time, a half inch off the bed.

The man leaned over and put one hand on either side

of Matt's neck. Face-to-face like this, Matt could see that he was young, that he had a chicken pox scar on his forehead. Was he a doctor? Or some kind of medic?

He turned Matt's head ever so slightly, and a sharp, hot stab of pain shot down his neck—pain so intense, it brought tears to Matt's eyes.

"That hurts." The man sounded pleased. "Good. Pain is good. Better than the alternative."

He made some notes on a clipboard. "Probable TBI," he said, almost to himself. Then he looked up at Matt. "Traumatic brain injury." He frowned, hurriedly making more notes. "I'll order up some tests for language retrieval, cognitive functioning."

Panic washed over Matt as he strained to understand. Cognitive problems? What did that mean? He tried to speak, but the doctor, or whatever he was, was already on his way out of the ward. Matt wanted to ask what had happened to him. To ask about the other guys in his squad. And to ask him to please, please bring him some water.

But a powerful weariness pressed down on him. He fought to keep it at bay, blinking once, then once more. Then he closed his eyes and surrendered to it.

The noises in the room—the hum of voices, the steady beep of a machine nearby, the faint trill of a phone—all faded to a low drone and for a moment, before he lost consciousness, Matt saw a little Iraqi boy standing at the end of an alley.

The alley was littered with debris. There was an overturned car in the middle of the street, a candy wrapper fluttering from a coil of razor wire, a stray dog nosing through a pile of trash. From far away, the high-pitched wail of the muezzin pierced the air, calling the faithful to prayers. There was a sudden, silent flash of light and the boy was lifted off his feet. He was smiling, smiling and slowly paddling his arms like a swimmer. Then he seemed to float, high up into the crayon-blue sky, until all Matt could see were the soles of his shoes as he disappeared, far above the burning city.

"ON BEHALF OF THE PRESIDENT OF THE UNITED STATES AND the citizens of a grateful nation . . ."

Matt opened his eyes and saw an officer, a lieutenant colonel, a man with a deeply tanned face and a regulation crew cut, standing over his bed. The man was clutching a box, the kind of thing that would hold a piece of jewelry, a necklace maybe. Then he took the thing from the box, leaned over, and laid it on Matt's chest.

He paused for a moment and searched Matt's eyes

for some sign of understanding. A heavy fatigue pressed down on Matt, but he struggled to keep his eyes open. He could feel the man's hands working as he took hold of the blanket and did something with it.

"I award you the medal of the Purple Heart," he heard the man say. "For wounds sustained in combat."

A Purple Heart. Matt had heard that the biggest, bravest, most badass guys in the army often burst into tears when that medal was pinned on their chests. But Matt didn't want a medal. He just wanted to know what was wrong with him. He felt his mouth flopping open and closed, gulping like a fish, but no sound came out.

"Your mission now, son, is to get better," the man said.

Matt tried to nod, to say, "Yes, sir," but nothing happened.

"Get better—and get back out there."

Again, the fatigue bore down on him, pushing him below the surface of consciousness, and he fell back into a thick, hazy sleep as he heard the man's footsteps echoing across the marble floor as he walked away.

WHEN MATT AWOKE, A PALE SHAFT OF LIGHT WAS STREAMING in from a window nearby. It was dusk, he decided. The light was too weak to be morning light. Dusk. Definitely dusk.

A few rows away, an army chaplain was praying silently over a figure in a bed. Matt tried to call out to him, but the sounds that came out of his mouth were sluggish and dull, not really words at all. The chaplain made the sign of the cross over the figure, then came and stood next to Matt.

The man had watery blue eyes and a cross-hatching of wrinkles that fanned out toward his temples. He was wearing an Oakland A's baseball cap, camouflage fatigues with a cross insignia, and some kind of purple scarf draped around his neck. The scarf had a special name. Matt knew it from his days as an altar boy. But he couldn't remember it.

The priest reached for the cup of water next to Matt's bed and lifted it as if he were raising the chalice at Communion. Matt nodded weakly and the priest put the straw to his mouth. The water was stale and tepid; it had probably been sitting there forever. But it felt good going down Matt's throat.

He took a few sips, then let his head fall back onto the pillow. "Father," he said, his voice cracking, "what's wrong with me?"

"I'm not sure I can answer that, son," the priest said. "Why don't we take a look at your chart?"

He walked to the foot of the bed and picked up a clipboard that must have been hanging there. "Says here you're eighteen years old. Catholic. Blood type O positive." The priest scanned the page silently. "They brought you in six hours ago. A couple of stitches, bruised ribs." He paused. "TBI. Traumatic brain injury."

Matt fought to stay calm. "What's that?"

"Laymen's terms? It's when your brain gets shaken up."

"I'm not . . ." The word was right on the tip of his tongue, but he couldn't remember it.

"Brain damaged?"

Matt nodded.

"Well, son, I'm not a doctor, but I think you're going to be fine."

"Why? How do you know?"

The priest sighed. "If your injury were more serious, they'd fly you out to Germany. In this war, as soon as you're well enough to walk and fire a gun, they send you back out. Evidently, they think you're going to be ready

7

to fight again before long."

Matt exhaled. If he could get back to the guys, everything would be okay.

The priest—the name stitched on his pocket said *Fr. Brennan*—opened his prayer book and began reciting something, his lips barely moving, his voice hushed. When he finished, he made the sign of the cross, then touched the tip of his purple scarf to Matt's forehead.

Matt's throat clamped up. What was wrong with him? When did he turn into such a crybaby? He bit down on the inside of his mouth to keep from crying.

The priest looked at him with what seemed like infinite understanding. "Be still, son," he said. "Be still. And know."

Matt had been expecting some kind of standard Catholic saying about the Lord being his shepherd, that sort of thing. "What's that from, sir?" he asked.

The priest smiled, took off his baseball cap, and held it out toward Matt. Under the brim, written in ballpoint pen, were the words: *Be still. And know.*

Matt didn't get it.

"It's short for 'Be still and know that I am in you and I do the work.'" Father Brennan stared down at the inscription. "Barry Zito. Oakland A's. Cy Young winner 2002."

Matt nodded.

"It's his mantra," Father Brennan said, wringing the cap in his hands. "Wrote it on the inside of his brim one time when he was in a slump. So when he got on the mound, he could just look up, see those words and tune out everything else. Turned his whole season around."

Matt remembered, sort of.

"Here in Iraq, the things you see, sometimes you wonder about God," Father Brennan said. He put his cap back on his head and walked toward the next bed. "But there's always baseball."

MATT LAY IN BED FOR A WHILE, TRYING TO TAKE IN HIS surroundings. Only a few of the other beds were filled and the people in them seemed to be sleeping or reading. There was an Alabama football bumper sticker plastered on the wall across from his bed. *Roll on, Tide*, it said. Matt wondered what happened to the soldier who'd put it there. Was he home, recovering? Or was he back with his squad? Or dead? Nearby was a magazine picture of Jessica Simpson in cut-off jeans and a straw hat. Someone had drawn words coming out of her mouth: *I support the troops.*

Matt thought for a minute of the bombed-out elementary school that their squad used as a base, where he had taped up a picture of Jennifer Lopez over his cot. Justin had written a bubble coming out JLo's mouth that said, *Matt Duffy is charismatic. Charismatic* was one of the words from Justin's word-a-day calendar, something his mom had sent him. The guys gave him endless grief about his vocabulary-improvement plan, but Justin was dead serious about it. "Just because I'm devastatingly handsome doesn't mean I can't also be smart," he'd said. On the bottom of the picture, Wolf, another one of the guys, had scribbled another line coming out of JLo's mouth: *I want Matt Duffy to be my baby daddy.*

"Mind if I take your vitals?" A young black woman in scrubs had appeared out of nowhere. Her skin was dark as blue velvet and her hair was pulled up into two bunches on the top of her head. She had wide, deep brown eyes and a full mouth. Her teeth stuck out a little, not in a rabbity way but in a way that was, for some reason Matt couldn't quite figure out, sort of sexy.

She laid a cool hand on Matt's wrist.

"Where am I?" he said.

She scarcely glanced up. "Ward twelve, bed thirty-seven."

"No, I mean, are we in Baghdad?" he said. "This place is pretty quiet." There was no shelling or AK-47 fire.

"Yup," she said. "Welcome to the Green Zone."

The famous Green Zone. The walled compound inside Baghdad where Saddam Hussein had once lived. Now it was occupied by the Central Provisional Authority. The brass.

Matt and his squad had patrolled Sadr City, an insurgent hotbed just outside the walls of the compound. But they'd all been fascinated with the Green Zone. Justin said the staff at the CPA could get hamburgers and hot showers there. "They can even watch movies in Saddam's old palace theater," he'd said one morning when they were on latrine cleanup duty. "America on the Tigris," Justin called it.

The nurse strapped a blood-pressure cuff on his arm and began squeezing the little black pump. "This used to be a private hospital for Saddam's friends."

Matt took a good look around. The walls and floors were covered in thickly veined gray-and-white marble. There was a crescent and star symbol inlaid in the floor in the center of the room. And everywhere there were little white signs in the curvy, mysterious alphabet of Arabic; underneath, in Magic Marker, were English labels.

Behind the nurse, Matt could see a fire extinguisher hanging on the wall. Next to it was a small plastic sign in Arabic, illustrated with a simple diagram of how to use it. A piece of duct tape had been stuck over the sign and someone had written on it, in English, *Fire Extinguisher*.

But the staff, or maybe the patients, had done their best to make the place look like home, too. There was a cluster of little desktop American flags at the nurses' station, a Rambo poster taped on the men's room door, and a wall covered with bumper stickers. *It's God's Job to Forgive Saddam. It's Our Job to Arrange the Meeting*, said one. *Proud to be an Infidel*, said another. And, down at the bottom, one about Bush: *He put the DUH in W.*

"Do you know what happened to the other guys in my squad?" he said.

If she'd heard, she didn't answer. She had released the blood-pressure cuff and was standing still as if she was listening for something. Then came the unmistakable *whoomp, whoomp* sound of helicopters in the distance.

"Medevacs," she said. And, just as quickly as she'd appeared, she left.

LATER, MATT DIDN'T KNOW HOW MUCH LATER, THE MAN IN the green scrubs came back to his bedside. This time, he was wearing a Stars and Stripes surgical cap. And this time, Matt had a chance to look at his name tag. *J. Kwong. M.D.* So he was a doctor, after all.

"Well, Private Duffy. It's been almost twenty-four hours," he said, looking down at Matt's chart. "How are you feeling?"

"Sir, what's this brain thing I have?" Matt said.

"TBI?" The doctor glanced up. "Most common injury in Iraq. It's like a concussion, only worse."

Matt waited for him to say more.

"We're going to keep you here for a couple days, do an evaluation," he said, making a note on the chart. "TBI usually gets better on its own—especially in mild cases. But it can get worse a couple days after the impact." He hung the clipboard at the foot of the bed. "We're going to keep an eye on you, get you up and moving, see what you remember, what you don't."

Matt nodded as if he understood. He didn't remember what Dr. Kwong had told him yesterday. He wasn't even sure he remembered what he'd said just a few minutes ago.

Dr. Kwong shined a light in Matt's eyes, then asked him if he knew what day it was.

Matt stared at him blankly.

"You know the month?"

Matt couldn't answer.

"The name of your unit?"

"The hundred-and-third."

Dr. Kwong made a note in his chart. "So," he said,

"here's what you can expect. Dizziness, memory problems . . ."

He went on with the checklist of symptoms, at the same time putting Matt's body through a series of motions—bending his legs, tapping his knees with a little rubber-tipped hammer, poking and prodding him.

". . . vomiting, problems with coordination, mood swings, low frustration threshold." He paused. "You may find yourself . . . agitated."

"Agitated?" Matt said. "What do you mean, 'agitated'?"

Dr. Kwong glanced away for a moment. "You may be . . . emotional for a while."

Matt looked away, too, focusing instead on a blond nurse who was changing the sheets on a bed across the way.

"You may have trouble remembering simple words and phrases," Kwong said. "And you could have a hard time learning and retaining new information."

"Sir," Matt said, "I have a . . ." He stopped.

"You don't have to call me sir."

"Thank you, sir," he said. "You know. When your head hurts. And you take aspirin . . ."

"Headache?" Dr. Kwong said.

"Yeah, a headache."

The doctor nodded. "Exactly what I'm talking about.

Difficulty with language retrieval." He looked up from the chart where he was making notes. "You follow hockey?"

Was this a trick question, Matt wondered, like asking him what day it was?

"Eric Lindros. Remember him?" Dr. Kwong was smiling now. "Played for the Philadelphia Flyers."

Matt tried to imagine what some hockey player from Philadelphia had to do with him.

"He had something like fifty concussions," Dr. Kwong said. "He has TBI."

"Oh," Matt said.

"Don't worry," Dr. Kwong said. "He also has a really hot wife." He scribbled a few more notes on the chart. Then closed the file.

"Someone from Lieutenant Colonel Fuchs's staff will come by later," the doctor said. "They'll ask you some questions. Write up a report about the incident." He hung the chart at the foot of the bed. "It's routine under these kinds of circumstances."

Matt didn't quite follow. *These kinds of circumstances?*

But the doctor was gone, his beeper summoning him somewhere else in the hospital.

MATT JERKED AWAKE WHEN A HAND TOUCHED HIS SHOULDER.

"Dude." The voice was familiar, but the face was a blur.

Matt stared, his eyes wide. First, he saw the glasses—the thick, nerdy-cool black glasses—then a thin, angular face. It was Justin. He was wearing his ACUs, the standard desert camouflage uniform, but he looked small somehow, deflated, without his helmet and his M16 slung over his shoulder.

"Dude," Justin said. "I was starting to think maybe I'd get Caroline's phone number after all."

Caroline. Matt had a picture of her taped inside his helmet, something Justin always teased him about. "I don't understand how a skinny little dude like you has such a hot girlfriend," he'd say. Matt put these bits of information together like beads on a string and he tried to understand if Justin was making a joke. He searched Justin's face.

But Justin was looking away, across the room at the soldier with the missing hand. He shook his head, then slowly turned his gaze toward Matt, his expression almost tender. He took hold of the blanket that had been

16

laid across Matt's chest and tucked it gently under his chin. Then he went to the foot of the bed, lifted Matt's feet carefully, and tucked the blanket snugly underneath them. It was the same thing Matt's mom used to do when he was little.

It was strange having Justin baby him like this, embarrassing—and again, tears pooled in Matt's eyes. He blinked them back, but a single tear slid down the side of his face and trickled into his ear.

Justin pretended he hadn't seen. He sat down, cleared his throat, then reached down to his leg and fiddled with the Velcro strap that held his father's knife from Vietnam. "It's a good thing you were so ugly to begin with."

"Am I . . ." Matt put a hand to his face. "Do I . . ."

"Relax, butthead." Justin cocked his chin in the direction of Matt's face. "You're fine. You've got a black eye, but to tell you the truth, it's actually an improvement."

Matt smiled. It hurt to smile.

"Oh, yeah," Justin said. "And a fat lip."

A nurse in green scrubs went by. She had a blond ponytail and a hot body and she reminded Matt of the blond girl from the Archie comic books. Betty. Or maybe Veronica? Justin followed her with his eyes until she turned the corner and was out of sight. He made an obscene gesture, pushing his tongue into the inside of his cheek.

"Congenial," he said. "That nurse is very congenial."

Matt smiled weakly. *Congenial*. Probably one of Justin's word-a-day words. Justin was famous for using the words the wrong way, but that didn't stop him. "Use a word ten times and it's yours," he'd say.

Justin's expression turned serious. "I thought you were a goner, man," he said. "You were on the business end of an RPG. Do you remember that?"

RPG. Rocket-propelled grenade. Matt nodded. But he didn't remember. Not at all. "Did . . ." He had to struggle to speak. "Did anyone else"—he swallowed—"get hurt?"

Justin looked down at his lap and rubbed his palm over his buzz cut—short, straight, blond hair that reminded Matt of fresh-mown hay. After a minute, he looked up at Matt.

"You don't remember?"

Matt shook his head. Even that tiny gesture sent pain shooting through his skull.

"It was yesterday," Justin said. "Remember yesterday?"

Matt tried to remember. Nothing.

"You sure?" Justin glanced over his shoulder, the way he did when he was scanning the rooftops for snipers. "Nothing at all?"

"Why? Did someone get hurt?"

18

Justin pinched his brow between his fingers. "Only a couple hajis," he said.

"Enemy" was the official term. "Insurgents" was okay, too. Everybody called them hajis, though. And unless your squad leader was a hard-ass, you could get away with it.

"Okay," Justin said, leaning in so close, Matt could smell the sweat and stink of him, the whiff of burned cordite that clung to their uniforms when they came back from a battle. "Okay, dude. I'll tell you what happened."

Justin straightened his glasses. "We were working the south checkpoint."

Matt nodded. They'd manned that checkpoint all week.

"And a taxi busts through the barricade . . ." Justin said.

"I remember that," Matt said. "Three guys in an orange-and-white taxi."

". . . So we jump in the Humvee and chase the bastards." Justin was hyped, the way he always was after a firefight. "We go down the street where that guy sells bootleg videos. It was like Grand Theft Auto, dude, taking the corners on two wheels."

Matt nodded. He remembered the bootleg guy; he had sold them a copy of *Spider-Man 3*. And he could picture the taxi disappearing around a corner, off the main road and down a side street. But he couldn't picture the rest of the squad. "Where were McNally and Wolf and the others?"

Justin narrowed his eyes and tucked his chin in toward his chest. "You don't remember?" he said.

Matt just looked at him.

"We got separated."

"Oh," Matt said.

"So we end up in an alley," Justin said. "And the bastards jump out of their car and disappear inside a house at the far end of the street. So we jump out of the Humvee and take off on foot. As soon as we do, we start taking fire."

Matt could picture the alley. It was like a million streets in Baghdad, a moonscape of dust and rubble, coils of razor wire rolling around on the ground like tumbleweeds. There was an overturned car in the middle of the street. And a dog. A mangy thing with a broken tail nosing through a pile of trash—right in the middle of a firefight.

"So we duck inside this house across the street," Justin said.

Matt could picture Justin running across the alley with his head down, but he had no recollection of a house.

"We find an upstairs window. We rip down the curtains and we see, across the street, at the other end, this one haji bastard leaning out the window trying to get a bead on our location," he said. "And so I light him up. Bam! He goes down like a ton of bricks."

"Wow," Matt said. "But how . . ."

"And then we're leaving, we're back on the street heading for the Humvee, and whoosh! Out of nowhere, an RPG slams into the wall about twenty feet away. You go flying, man. Then you hit the ground and I have to haul you out of there by the straps on your vest."

He reached over and took hold of the front of Matt's hospital gown as if he were grabbing hold of him by the straps of his vest. Then he let go and patted Matt on the cheek. "You were lucky, man."

"There was a dog," Matt said.

Justin frowned. "What?"

"Dog," said Matt. "There was a dog."

Justin drew back slightly. "Dude, I have no idea what the fuck you're talking about."

"He was near the . . . you know, when you throw stuff away . . ." It was maddening. He couldn't remember the word.

Justin looked away, scanning the room.

"The dog!" Matt punched the mattress with his fist. "He had a broken tail."

Justin stood up. He seemed to be gesturing for someone.

Matt jerked his head to the side, to see who Justin was calling for. A bolt of pain shot through his skull. He clenched his head and cried out in agony.

Now the nurse with the blond ponytail was standing over the bed. She wasn't pretty after all, Matt thought as she went to work checking the IV in his arm, readying a syringe and then methodically emptying the contents of the syringe into his IV tube. Matt caught a glimpse of Justin over her shoulder, but Justin wouldn't look at him. He was studying a hangnail as if it were the most important thing in the world.

That was the last thought Matt had before he fell, headlong, into a foggy, restless sleep.

A FEMALE OFFICER—A YOUNGISH WOMAN IN A UNIFORM SKIRT—came by a little later, carrying a satellite phone. She was cute, but she was all business. Like a lot of women in the army, she had that don't-mess-with-me look on her face. She'd be pretty, Matt thought, if she weren't making that stupid face. She had reddish hair, a turned-up nose, and small, delicate ears.

"You get to make a call home," she said briskly. "You need to call so they can put out the press release."

Matt just looked at her.

"They have to notify next of kin before they can put out a statement about the incident."

"Oh," he said.

"As you know, the army prohibits the release of specific information—dates, places, et cetera." She'd obviously given this speech a few times.

"But I don't know what happened," Matt said.

"Well then, it shouldn't be a very long call." She handed him the phone and stood there while he dialed.

He heard a rapid series of computerized beeps as the satellite processed the number. There was a pause, then the oddly quaint sound of the phone ringing. He imagined the squat little ranch house where he'd grown up, the cordless phone with the broken antenna in the kitchen, the speckled linoleum floor, the dishrag hung on the oven door, the milkmaid figurines his mom collected.

His sister picked up the phone on the first ring. "Hello?" she said. "Brandon?"

"Lizzy?" he said. "It's Matt."

"Oh." She sounded surprised and maybe a tiny bit disappointed. "I thought you were going to be Brandon."

"Lizard," Matt said, "what time is it there?" It could

be the middle of the day or the middle of the night, for all he knew.

"I don't know. Eleven thirty, maybe."

"So what's Brandon doing calling so late at night?"

"Jeez, Matt, when did you turn into such a tool?" She snapped her gum.

It was funny, Matt thought, how the tiny sound of a piece of Bubblicious popping in the United States could travel all the way to the other side of the world in a millisecond. "Is he treating you good? Brandon?" he said.

The cute red-haired officer leaned over and tapped her watch.

"Liz," Matt said, "get Mom, okay?"

"You okay?" Her tone was suddenly serious.

"Of course, just go get her." He could hear the phone clatter onto the table as Lizzy yelled, "Ma. It's Matty." And he could picture his mom running to pick up the phone, grabbing her cigarettes off the counter on her way.

She was out of breath and, he could tell, scared. Whenever he called home, she sounded like she was bracing for bad news. He'd told her, over and over again, that if something really bad happened to him, the army wouldn't call; they'd send someone to the house. But the first words out of her mouth were always the same: "Is everything okay?"

"Ma?" he said. "It's me."

"Oh, Jesus, Matt. Is everything okay? Where are you?"

"Yeah, Ma, I'm fine. . . ."

"Are you . . ."

". . . Just got a little banged up."

". . . all in one piece?"

There was a slight delay in the line, so they talked over each other, then paused and waited for the other one, then started talking again at the same time.

"Go ahead," he said.

"No, you go ahead."

"I'm okay. I just, you know, got a bump on the head. I'm in, you know, the infirmary, but I'm good," he said.

The female officer who'd given him the phone stood by, listening in, as Matt hemmed and hawed about what had happened. He said it was no big deal, just another day in Iraq.

"Are you sure?" He could hear his mother's voice cracking.

"Ma! If I say I'm fine, I'm fine." He hadn't meant to yell at her. Yelling also made his head throb. "Look," he said, a little more gently, "they told me I'll be back with my squad in a couple days."

"Oh." Her voice sounded little and far away. She *was* little and far away, Matt thought. Little and far away and all by herself. His dad had split a long time ago. Which

25

meant there was no money for college for Lizzy, who, unlike Matt, was really good in school. When Matt came home from the recruiter's office, his mom had cried. When he said now she'd have college money for Lizzy, she'd cried even harder.

They were quiet for a minute, then they both started talking at the same time.

"How's Caroline?" he said.

". . . markers you wanted," she said.

"What did you say?" he said.

"What did you say?" she said.

"I asked if you've seen Caroline lately."

"I said I sent those colored markers you asked for," she said. "For the little Iraqi boy."

"Oh," they both said at the same time.

The officer tapped her watch again, and Matt was actually glad to have an excuse to hang up.

"I gotta go, Ma," Matt said. "I'll write. If you see Caroline, tell her I'm okay. Okay?"

"I also sent you peanut butter," his mom said. "And more socks."

"That's great, Ma. You're the greatest," he said. "So you'll tell Caroline, right?"

"And cookies. Snickerdoodles. The kind you like."

"Ma," he said, "I gotta go."

". . . just hope they don't get all broken . . ."

The last time his mom sent cookies, all that arrived was a box of crumbs. He'd told her they were delicious, that the guys loved them.

"Okay, Ma," he said. He cupped his free hand over the receiver. "I love you, Ma," he whispered.

He looked up and saw the female officer smiling, just a little, despite herself.

Then he heard a tiny sniffling sound, then a few muted beeps as they were disconnected.

THE HEAVY *THUMP-THUMP* OF A BOOM-BOX BEAT WOKE HIM up sometime later. Matt looked around, not sure where he was for a moment. It was midmorning, he figured, judging by the slant of the sunlight streaming in through an open window. The music—50 Cent—was blasting from outside.

He sat up gingerly, his whole body stiff and sore, then eased himself to the side of the bed and looked out his second-story window. He could see the gold dome of a mosque in the distance and the city skyline fringed with palm trees. Directly below his window was a dusty lot where a bunch of Iraqi kids were dancing. A gangly little boy stood in the center of the group, lip-synching and wagging his hands in a spot-on imitation of a rapper.

"I'll take you to the candy shop . . ." the kid pretended to sing. "I'll let you lick the lollipop."

It was unreal, seeing this skinny, barefoot kid doing a hand glide, and Matt thought about what Justin had said once when they were in the street handing out candy to the scrum of little kids who followed them everywhere: "We're bringing these people America!"

For nearly a month after Matt's squad had first arrived, there'd been a lull in the fighting, so his squad was instructed to establish contacts within the community. He and Justin had pulled a couple Humvees and Bradleys into a circle and made a soccer field. Then they gathered a bunch of kids who'd been picking through the trash heap next to their base, looking for tin cans to sell for salvage, and organized them into two teams: the Weapons of Mass Destruction and the Shock and Awe. Justin played with the Shock and Awe kids and Matt with the WMDs. The kids ran around barefoot on the hard, littered patch of ground, but they still outmaneuvered the two soldiers.

As he gazed out the window, Matt pictured Ali, a ten-year-old who was one of the WMDs, scoring a goal, running away from the net. Usually Ali celebrated by spreading his arms like a pair of airplane wings, like the great Brazilian forward, Ronaldo. It was a move he'd picked up watching TV in the market, as he knelt on the ground and peeked through the forest of men's legs.

But if it was an especially pretty goal, he'd look over at Matt and make an imaginary pair of glasses around his eyes with his fingers.

The gesture had two meanings. It meant "Did you see that?" But it was also a reference to Matt's shiny wrap-around sunglasses. The ones Ali had stolen the first day they'd met.

He'd come up to Matt one day in the market and tugged on his jacket. "Hello, Skittles," he'd said, running the two words together as if Matt's name was Skittles.

Matt had no candy left, but the kid was so skinny—his belly was bloated and he had legs like a stork—that Matt started digging around in his pockets for an energy bar. He gave Ali his sunglasses to hold for a minute. Next thing he knew, the boy had run off with them. The glasses, which Matt's mom had given him, were absolutely cru-cial in the brutal Iraqi sun and so Matt had chased after him until he disappeared around a corner.

But he couldn't catch him, something for which Charlene, their civil affairs officer, had given him mer-ciless grief. "How are we gonna find weapons of mass destruction if you can't even find a pair of shades?" she'd said.

Girls—females, as the army called them—weren't

29

technically allowed in combat, but Charlene had been "attached" to their squad to conduct searches of females after the army found out that some of the enemy soldiers were dressing as women to avoid being searched. For a civil affairs officer, though, she didn't seem to actually like civilians all that much. And she seemed to take some satisfaction in this kid running off with Matt's glasses. "See?" she said in a schoolteachery tone. "That's what happens when you try to make friends with these people."

Later that day, the chaplain stopped by and said Mass. It was outside, in the town square, and Matt noticed the same kid standing there, watching as the soldiers went up to receive Communion. Then the boy got in line—he copied the way people folded their hands and bowed their heads—and he stuck his tongue out. The priest didn't bat an eye. And the boy chewed the tiny wafer like he couldn't get it down fast enough. A few minutes later he was back in line, for seconds.

When Mass ended and Matt stood up from the crate he was sitting on, the sunglasses were on the ground behind him.

Outside, the boom box went silent. One of the kids jiggled it and it stuttered to life again, then died. The group started to disperse, then one of kids ran to a corner of the lot and retrieved a soccer ball. One of the Stars and

Stripes soccer balls the troops handed out.

The kids sorted themselves into two teams and began tearing around the lot. One kid—a barefoot boy in a pair of shorts and a T-shirt—darted in and out, then scored a goal, placing his shot between an empty Gatorade bottle and a rock that served as goalposts. Then he ran away from the net, his arms outstretched.

The boy slowed down, then drifted out of the heat into the shade under Matt's window. He bent over, caught his breath, and then a moment later stepped out into the sunshine to return to the field.

Matt watched, but in his mind, he saw Ali. Ali stepping out from the shade of a doorway and into bright light. The image made his mouth go dry.

LATER, MATT DECIDED TO SEE IF HE COULD WALK A LITTLE bit. The sooner he could get better, the sooner he'd be back with the guys.

He used his arms to push himself off the bed, and he took a few shaky steps. Then his knees wobbled and he felt himself sinking. He leaned back against the bed.

"Easy there, cowboy." It was the pretty black nurse who'd taken his blood pressure.

Matt grabbed the back of his hospital gown to make sure it was tied. Then he took another timid step forward. He teetered there a moment, then his right leg gave out and he had to grab the handrails on the bed to keep from falling down.

"I think maybe that's enough for today," she said, turning him back toward the bed with a strength that surprised him.

Her breasts were practically at eye level as she helped him into bed and he turned his face sideways so she wouldn't think he was taking advantage of the situation. She smelled good, like baby powder.

"Thanks," he said after he was back in bed. "Thanks, Nurse McCrae." Her name tag had also been right at eye level.

She left, then came back a minute later carrying a gray army T-shirt, a pair of black gym shorts, and some rubber flip-flops. "Here," she said. "In case you want to go for another walk."

"SO WHAT HAPPENED TO YOU?"

Matt had attempted a second walk. This time, he made it as far as two cots away, where a beefy soldier with broad cheeks, jet-black hair cut in a flattop, and dark, almost crimson skin was scribbling rapidly in a notebook. He hardly glanced up from his writing when Matt stopped at the foot of his bed to rest a moment. Matt stood there, too winded to answer.

"You got any Percocet?" the guy said.

Percocet. Matt didn't know what that was. Or he had known, a long time ago, but couldn't remember.

"Percs, Oxy. Whatever," the guy said. "Bennies, even. I'll give you five bucks. Or three packs of Marlboros."

Matt understood that it was his turn to say something, but he didn't know how to answer. "I don't have those things," he said finally. He was embarrassed at the way he sounded: stilted, almost babyish. The other soldier knotted his thick, dark eyebrows, then went back to writing in his notebook.

Matt considered walking to his bed, but it seemed very far away. He cleared his throat and looked at the other soldier; he was powerfully built, tall a good foot taller than Matt—and several years older, too.

"What happened to you?" Matt said. "Why are you here?"

The guy looked up, assessing Matt. "Bad case of CFU."

"CFU?"

"Completely fucked up."

Matt nodded as if he understood. The other guy looked him over head to toe, seemed to make a decision about him, then stuck out his hand. "Francis."

Matt nodded again, not quite sure what to do next.

"How 'bout you?" Francis said. "You got a name?"

"Duffy," he said. "Matt."

Francis closed his notebook partway, keeping his finger inside at the page where he'd been writing, and gestured for Matt to sit down. Behind him, on his pillow, was a stuffed animal—a tattered Miss Piggy doll. Francis pushed Miss Piggy aside to make room. "It's my daughter's," he said. "She's five."

Matt eased himself onto the edge of the bed, surprised by how much a relief it was to sit down. Francis was wearing a gray army T-shirt and black basketball shorts just like the ones Nurse McCrae had given Matt. There didn't seem to be a scratch anywhere on him.

"Yup," Francis said. "Absolutely nothing wrong with me."

Matt didn't know what to say.

Francis tapped his temple with his finger. "Head case," he said.

Matt felt himself pull back ever so slightly.

If Francis noticed, he didn't let on. "So what brings you here, Duffy Matt?"

Matt frowned. He couldn't remember the name of

34

the thing that happened to his brain. It was three initials. "My brain got shook up," he said finally.

Francis nodded. "IED?"

Matt shook his head. It wasn't an IED. He knew what that was: an improvised explosive device. A roadside bomb.

Sergeant Benson, their first squad leader, had been killed by an IED. Tore his left leg off. While the rest of the squad covered the body with a blue plastic tarp, Justin had taken off on his own. They were always supposed to travel in pairs and it was standard operating procedure to stick together after an attack, to set up a defensive position in case there was a second attack. But Justin had stormed off to a nearby tea shop to ask questions. He came back, pushing an old man in front of him, his M16 pressed into the man's back. "I found this on him," Justin had said, tossing a cell phone into the dirt.

The insurgents often used cell-phone signals to detonate bombs, but the old man didn't have the hard, defiant look of an enemy fighter. He was crying and plucking at his beard; Matt could see he'd wet his pants.

The old man fell to his knees and started kissing Justin's boots. As Justin stared at the man huddled at his feet, his expression changed slowly from disbelief to disgust. Justin was about to kick the man, Matt realized.

Without thinking, Matt had thrown himself between

Justin and the old man, taking Justin to the ground in a flying tackle. The two of them wrestled around in the dirt, throwing furious, clumsy punches at each other until, finally, Matt had him pinned. "I know you loved Benson," Matt said. "And I know you're pissed. But this isn't the time to do something stupid."

That night the squad had had to sleep on the floor of an Iraqi home, huddled together to stay warm. Matt woke up in the middle of the night to find Justin covering him with a thin blanket he must have found somewhere in the house. Then Justin lay down next to him, cradling his rifle in his arms, and closed his eyes. They never said a word about what had happened that day, but after that they had become inseparable.

"Kid!" Francis snapped his fingers in front of Matt's eyes. "Was it an IED?"

Matt shook his head. "It was something else," he said. He closed his eyes for a second, concentrating hard. He pictured Justin sitting next to his hospital bed. "I was on the business end of an RPG," he said finally.

Francis whistled. "You in pain?"

Matt shook his head. A dull ache pulsed at the base of his skull. "Some," he said.

Francis reached under his pillow and pulled out a plastic bottle of pills. "I'm out of codeine," he said. "But I got plenty of these." It was Ripped Fuel, a capsule a lot of the guys took before they went out on all-night patrols. It had something in it called ephedra, which Justin said had more caffeine than a hundred packs of Nescafé crystals. But Matt didn't like it; it made him jumpy.

"No thanks," he said.

Francis scanned the ward. Only a few beds were occupied. Down at one end, two guys were playing poker, using cigarettes for chips. Across the aisle, one guy was showing his tattoo to the guy in the next bed. Francis downed a couple of capsules without water, then turned to Matt.

"You keeping a journal?" he said. He tapped the black notebook in his hand but didn't wait for Matt to answer. "Everything goes in here. Every order I got, every raid I went on."

"How come?"

"They're going to question you," he said. "Everybody here gets interviewed. About, you know, what happened to them."

Matt frowned. "I don't know what happened to me."

"Well, you're gonna want to figure that out," Francis said.

Then the doors at the end of the room swung open and a pair of MPs came striding in. The ward fell silent.

There was a lot to be afraid of in Iraq: roadside bombs, snipers, mortar fire. But seeing a pair of military police coming toward you was just about the worst. It meant someone was in trouble with the brass. Big trouble. "I'd rather have a bunch of hajis shooting my ass off than deal with those assholes," Justin once said. "Those guys will make your life a living hell."

Matt averted his eyes as the two MPs advanced, but Francis shoved his notebook under his pillow and got out of bed.

"Sorry, brother," Francis said, turning toward Matt. "Looks like I have a date."

A STRANGE SOUND WOKE MATT IN THE MIDDLE OF THE NIGHT. At first, he thought it was the faint mewling of an alley cat. There were lots of strays in Baghdad, cats and dogs. His squad had adopted a tiny gray kitten they'd found nosing through the garbage during their first week in country. Itchy, they named him. The first time a mortar hit the compound, the soldiers had practically jumped out of their socks. Itchy didn't even blink. Only a few weeks old, he was already a veteran.

But as Matt listened more closely, he understood that the sound wasn't coming from outside. And it wasn't a kitten. It was a man, several beds away, weeping softly.

"WHAT DAY IS IT?"

Matt shrugged. "The doctor asked me that yesterday," he said. He was in a tiny office, sitting across the table from the cute young female officer who'd brought the satellite phone to him the other day. Her name was Meaghan, Meaghan Finnerty, and she had reddish-blond hair that she kept tucking behind her ears, ears that were small and pink. They reminded Matt of seashells.

The sign on her door—written in Magic Marker above an indecipherable Arabic word—said *Evaluations*.

"Do you know what month it is?" she said.

Matt didn't answer.

"Don't worry," she said. "This isn't a test. Your answers are confidential."

Matt sighed. September was Caroline's birthday, and he remembered Sergeant McNally giving him leave to go to the rear operating base to call her with his free USO calling card. It had been three in the morning her time, so Caroline was asleep. She said there'd been a fight at the homecoming game. That had been only a little while ago, so he took a guess. "October?"

Meaghan Finnerty didn't let on if this was right or

39

wrong. "How about the day of the week?"

Matt was pretty sure he'd been in the hospital for a day and a half, maybe two; he counted backward from when Dr. Kwong had said he'd been there for twenty-four hours and tried to remember how many times the orderlies had brought around the meal carts. That added up to two days, give or take, but he still had no idea what days.

He shrugged.

"Can you tell me the names of your squad members?" she said.

"Justin—he's my boy," Matt said. "Wolf—his real name is Hugh, but we call him that because of how he can howl. He has a wolf sticker on the back of his helmet. His mom sent us Silly String."

She nodded, her expression unreadable.

Matt went on, anxious to show her how much he could remember. "Sergeant McNally. He's from Pittsburgh. He's a . . . you know, when you stand on a ladder . . ." He kneaded his brow with the tips of his fingers. His head was throbbing and he couldn't think of the word. He looked at Meaghan Finnerty for help.

"Does he use a hammer or a paintbrush?" she asked.

"A hammer, ma'am. He makes things. Like shelves." The word was just out of reach.

"Is he a carpenter?"

"Yes, ma'am. A carpenter. That's it." He felt like a fool.

Meaghan Finnerty reached for a stack of what looked like playing cards. She held one up and asked him to tell her what it was.

"A shoe," he said in a sullen tone.

She held up another card.

It was the thing you wear when it rains. Matt bit his lip and tried to think of the word. Then he stood up abruptly, scattering Meaghan Finnerty's stack of cards all over the floor. He wasn't going to play this stupid, kindergarten game anymore.

"I'm not an idiot, you know." He waited for her to dress him down or kick him out of her office.

"I know you're not," she said simply.

"Then what's the matter with me?" He slumped back down in the chair, weak suddenly from his outburst, his head pounding.

"A lot of people with TBI have trouble finding or remembering words. And they often do what you did: use a complicated definition for a common item," she said. "It's a way of covering up for a lack of understanding or an inability to think of a word."

"Is that why I just acted like such an asshole?" He caught himself. "Ma'am. Excuse me, ma'am."

But Meaghan Finnerty smiled ever so slightly.

"That's a good sign."

"Acting like a . . . jerk?"

She shook her head and stray pieces of her hair came untucked from behind her ears. "Calling yourself one."

"I don't get it," Matt said.

"People with traumatic brain injury often have trouble with social situations; they can't seem to interpret the actions or feelings of others," she said. "At least you knew you were acting like an asshole."

This time, Matt smiled.

"Smiling. That's a good sign, too," she said. "A lot of people have difficulty understanding jokes or sarcasm or abstract expressions."

Matt swallowed. "Can you, you know, can you help me?" He couldn't believe it; he was near tears again. He needed to remember what happened in that alley. Someone was going to question him any day and all he knew was what Justin had told him. And he could hardly remember that. Worse, bits and pieces were coming back to him, things that made no sense.

"We'll do what we can here."

"What do you mean?" he said.

"If it turns out you need extensive help, they'll send you to Germany."

Iraq had felt terrifyingly strange when he'd first arrived; after only a few months, it was the only place he could imagine being. Now it was the idea of going to Germany—of leaving his buddies—that seemed terrifying.

"We'll know in another day or two," she said. "I'll evaluate you again and see if we can get you back out in the field."

Matt stared at her, his brow furrowed. He pictured himself standing in a meadow.

"We don't want you out in the field unless you're able to quickly process information, respond to orders, that sort of thing."

He nodded slowly, tentatively. It dawned on him: "Out in the field" was one of those abstract expressions she was talking about.

"But you have to be prepared . . ." she was saying. "You may have trouble concentrating. Especially when it comes to integrating new or complex pieces of information."

Matt knelt down, gathered up the picture cards on the floor, and handed them to her.

"Raincoat," he said as he turned to leave.

Meaghan Finnerty frowned.

"That last picture you showed me. It was a raincoat."

THE NURSE WITH THE FUZZY PIGTAILS CAME TO HIS BED THE
first thing the next morning, lugging a dusty green duffel
bag. "Your buddy dropped this off," she said, setting it on
the bed. "Private Kane."

"Justin?" Matt said. "Is he here?"

She shook her head. "He said you might want this
stuff," she said. Then one of the other nurses called out
for her and she walked away, her white shoes squeaking
with efficiency as she crossed the room.

Duct-taped to the bag was a note from Justin.

Dude,
You are still the baddest, cold-hard killer around—
even if you are wearing a little blue hospital gown
that shows your bare white ass. Good luck with the
sex change operation.
    Party on,
    J
    P.S. My dad can finally stop harping. Looks
like I'm going to get a medal for saving that nubile
white ass of yours.
    P.P.S. Charlene says you can borrow her nail
polish anytime.

Justin's dad was a Vietnam vet; he'd gotten a bunch of medals, including a Bronze Star with a V for valor. He was gung ho about the war, sending Justin letters saying how he'd better kill some hajis and bring home a medal. Justin didn't answer his letters; he said he wasn't going to write back until he had something to say that would shut his dad up. Matt smiled at the word *nubile*. An old word of the week.

And Charlene, who was only about five feet three but could bench-press more weight than half the guys in their battalion, was the biggest hard-ass in the group. "I'm in combat just as much as you guys are," she'd said, holding out a quarter-size piece of shrapnel she wore on a cord around her neck. "Souvenir of a firefight from March." The guys had given her merciless shit when she'd pulled a bottle of nail polish out of her duffel—until she showed them how to use it to repair a leak in the tube of her gas mask.

Matt tugged on the drawstring of his duffel bag. Stuffed inside were a couple pairs of clean underwear, a can of foot powder, his DVD player, along with the sixth season of *South Park*, his yearbook, a can of Pringles, and a packet of Skoal. At the bottom were his letters from Caroline folded inside a Ziploc bag, along with the picture he'd kept taped inside his helmet. He'd only been in the hospital for, what? forty-eight hours?, but the things in the duffel bag looked like souvenirs from another life, like the baby pictures and old report cards his mom kept in a scrapbook—especially the picture of Caroline.

It was a photo of her in her cheerleading uniform. She was looking off into the distance, at something that was happening on the football field, twirling a strand of hair around her finger. He had another picture of her—a photo of the two of them at the prom, standing under an arch covered in plastic flowers—but he liked this one best because she hadn't known her picture was being taken. She was just standing there, in front of everyone in the bleachers, unaware of how little-girlish she looked, twirling her hair around her finger, concentrating, trying to understand what had just happened on the field.

He slipped the picture out of the Ziploc bag and held it gingerly by the tips of his fingers. At night, before they went out on house-to-house searches, he'd take the picture out and spend the last few minutes before they left looking at Caroline twirling her hair, pretending he was in the bleachers watching her. He could practically feel the snap in the fall air, hear the shrill call of the referee's whistle, feel the lump in his jacket pocket where he'd hidden a can of Budweiser.

But now she seemed more like someone in one of those celebrity magazines. Her face was familiar—the way Jennifer Aniston or Britney Spears was familiar—in the way that makes you feel like you know the person, even though all you really know is their picture. He put the picture back in the Ziploc bag and slipped it under his pillow.

He opened the yearbook and flipped idly through the pages. He scanned the pictures of the debate team, the Honor Society, the Chemistry Club, and wondered what those kids were doing right now. *Go get Saddam*, one kid had written. *Remember the Alamo*, said another.

As he turned the page, a piece of paper fluttered onto the bed. It was a child's drawing of a battle. The guns— M16s and M4s—were precisely drawn, even though they were nearly as big as the soldiers. A Black Hawk UH-60 hovered overhead—complete with Hellfire antitank missiles mounted on the sides. Its guns spit out a shower of bullets—drawn as a hundred tiny pencil hash marks arching across on the paper. At the bottom it was signed in wobbly English letters: *Ali*.

The last time he'd seen Ali was when they were patrolling the market near the al-Hikma Mosque. Charlene had caught him trying to steal a blue plastic tarp off the back of their Humvee.

"Skittles," he said, batting his eyes at Charlene. "Please."

Ali had become a bit of a pest. He'd started out begging for food, but lately, he seemed to miraculously

47

appear whenever they were in his sector, hanging around, getting underfoot, begging for batteries, old magazines, empty soda cans—anything he could sell. Charlene had shooed him away, then turned to Matt. "We're really not supposed to fraternize with the local children."

Matt couldn't believe it. She was quoting from the new Army Field Manual. "We're here to help these people, Charlene. Besides, he's just a kid."

Matt picked up the drawing, studied it for a while, then tucked it inside the Ziploc bag along with Caroline's letters.

FRANCIS WAS BACK, WRITING FURIOUSLY IN A SMALL BLACK notebook. At the other end of the room, there was a new guy—a middle-aged man with soft, sloping shoulders and a bit of a paunch—sitting up in bed reading *Hustler*. Matt decided to go for another walk, to see if he could make it as far as that guy's bed.

He felt a little stronger this time, a little more steady on his feet, but he was aware that his right leg was dragging a little. It didn't hurt; it just didn't move in sync with his other leg. Two days and he was able to walk forty-five steps.

The guy turned the magazine upside down on his belly. "So," he said, "what brings you here?"

"I was on the business end of an RPG," Matt said. This phrase still didn't sound quite right, but it was the one thing he was sure of. "What about you?"

"Threw my back out hauling a drum of kerosene," he said. "I'm pretty sure they don't give out Purple Hearts for that. Too bad. I'd like to bring that back to my class."

Matt didn't get it.

"Shop class," the guy said. "I teach shop. I'm National Guard. Never thought they'd actually send us here. But I'll tell you, I am too old for this crap. I'll be forty-three next month and I am too old to be running around this godforsaken place, chasing after kids half my age, looking for hajis around every corner . . ."

An image—Justin bolting around a corner, running across the alley with his head down—flashed into Matt's mind, then vanished as quickly as it had come.

". . . but they need me, you know what I mean?" The shop teacher kept talking, unaware that Matt had stopped listening. "I can even rig up a DVD player to run off a car battery. What about you?" he said. "What do you do back home?"

"Me? Auto detailing."

"So the army gave you a big pay raise, right? Nine

hundred a month to get shot at. I bet you're not even legal to buy beer, am I right?"

Matt nodded.

Talking to this guy—or, rather, listening to him—was exhausting and Matt started to walk away, his head pounding.

He'd only gone about a half dozen steps when he had to stop and grab hold of the railing of an empty bed. He stood there as his legs trembled uncontrollably. The railing started to slip from his grasp—his hands were suddenly sweaty—and he felt his legs give out from under him.

A pair of hands grabbed him roughly, lifting him up by the armpits. It was Francis. Somehow he'd made it from the other end of the ward just in time.

"Whoa there, little buddy," he said. "Am I gonna have to tell the bartender to cut you off?"

Matt looked into his eyes. They were deep brown, the color of a strong cup of coffee.

Matt shook his head. "I don't even have a fake ID."

Francis whistled through his teeth. "Your brain really did get shook up, kid."

He helped Matt back to his bed, practically carrying him the last few yards, then turned back the covers and laid him down with a gentleness that shocked Matt.

"What did those MPs want with you?" Matt said as

50

Francis was about to leave.

Francis gazed out the window. "The truth?" he said, looking at some invisible point in the distance. "It's like Jack Nicholson said. You can't handle the truth."

MATT SAT IN BED FLIPPING THROUGH THE PAGES OF A BOOK of World Series trivia he'd found in the bathroom while the new guy in the bed across from him played with a yo-yo. Outside, he could hear the dull thrum of the hospital generator. A car drove by, its radio blaring a Middle Eastern tune—leaving a few quivering notes of the singer's voice in its wake.

He knew that song from somewhere. He put down the trivia book and stared at the bobbing yo-yo. But what he saw was a dusty alleyway. An overturned car. A candy wrapper snagged on a coil of razor wire. Bullets kicking up sparks on the pavement. A mangy dog with a crooked tail.

"They all sound the same, don't they?"

Matt blinked. The soldier with the yo-yo was talking to him. The man was sort of short, but he was well-built, with biceps so big, they stretched the sleeves of his T-shirt. His head was shaved clean and shaped like a

51

bullet and he had a tattoo on one arm that said *Mom*.

"Their songs," the guy said, not missing a beat as the yo-yo slid up and down on its string. "It's always some chick with a high voice yodeling."

As the last strains of the song died out, Matt thought again of the dusty alleyway. All of the alleys in Baghdad looked the same—piles of plaster where mortar rounds had hit the buildings, flat tires and abandoned car parts in the middle of the street, razor wire and graffiti everywhere. But right in the middle of all that chaos, all that destruction, you'd stumble on signs of family life—laundry flapping in the wind, a chicken pecking in a yard, a radio playing from somewhere inside.

"I know that song," Matt said flatly.

"What? You listen to that shit?" The guy had curled the yo-yo into his palm, stopping its rhythmic motion.

"No," said Matt. "Not really."

The guy swiveled a little so his back was almost facing Matt and he pointed to a spot on his shoulder. "Shot," he said. "By a sniper."

Matt nodded to show his appreciation. "So are they sending you to Germany?"

"No fucking way," he said. "They wanted to, but I told them 'fuck no.' Told them I was going to stay here and get better as fast as I can so I could get back out there with my boys."

"Oh." This guy was like Charlene: 110 percent committed to the mission. But he loved his squad, that was for sure.

Matt thought about his squad, about Justin, about Wolf and Figueroa, about their new squad leader, Sergeant McNally. The first thought that came to mind wasn't a firefight or a door-to-door search.

It was the time Wolf's mom sent him a bunch of cans of Silly String. The whole squad ran around the barracks, hiding and ambushing one another, spraying neon green Silly String everywhere, imitating the *ack-ack* sound of an M16 each time they fired. They were *playing* war, Matt remembered thinking, while a real one was raging outside.

As he watched Wolf squirt Silly String down the back of Figueroa's shirt, he remembered thinking, *This* is what war is all about. It wasn't about fighting the enemy. It wasn't about politics or oil or even about terrorists. It was about your buddies; it was about fighting for the guy next to you. And knowing he was fighting for you.

He thought about Itchy, wondering if the guys in his squad were taking care of him. He could picture them, on their cots inside the abandoned school that they were using as their base. At this time of night, Figueroa would be writing to his wife, Matt and Justin would be playing Halo, and Wolf would be cleaning his weapon or doing push-ups. And Itchy would be curled up in the shape of a comma at the foot of his cot, purring.

A SHADOW FELL OVER THE BED AND MATT OPENED HIS EYES TO see Francis standing above him, his leg twitching. "Here," he said, holding out what looked like a small paperback book. "I traded some Vicodin for it."

Matt studied the thing in his hand. It was a notebook with a picture of a basket of puppies on the front.

"I know," Francis said. "It's kind of 'Don't Ask, Don't Tell,' but it was all I could find. Got it off a nurse from Mobile."

Matt flipped through the empty pages of the book, not quite sure what he was supposed to do with it.

"Write down everything you know," Francis said. "Everything about what happened the day they brought you in here. When they bring you over to Fuchs's office, you'll at least have something."

And then Francis disappeared, leaving Matt sitting there, staring at the blank first page of the notebook. Fuchs's office. He struggled to remember who Fuchs was. Kwong had mentioned him. Was Fuchs the one who was going to question him, write up a report? Francis seemed pretty worked up about the whole thing. But Kwong had said it was routine under these circumstances. What did that mean?

There was so much Matt didn't know. He was in the hospital because of an RPG—Justin had told him that much. But he didn't remember anything about the attack. Kwong said it was because of that brain thing he had. And he said he might have trouble learning new information. So Matt made two lists: the things he did know and the things he didn't.

The list of things he didn't know included big things and small ones. The details of the attack. Where his squad was now. What exactly Francis had done to end up in trouble. When he'd last heard from Caroline. Where he'd seen that dog with the crooked tail.

When it came time to list the things he did know, he couldn't think of anything he knew for sure.

A LETTER FROM CAROLINE WAS SITTING ON HIS BEDSIDE TABLE when he woke up the next morning. The army, despite all the many ways it was screwed up, always managed to get the mail delivered—even when they were out in some nowhere town in Iraq. And now they'd forwarded the letter from his old barracks to the hospital.

He looked at the envelope. On the front someone had scrawled the name of the hospital. On the back was a message from Justin.

Figueroa says he's gonna eat all your mom's cookies if you don't get back soon. And Wolf says he wants your picture of JLo if you don't make it.

P.S. Fruit of the Month Club called; they want you to be Miss October.

Inside was Caroline's familiar writing.

Dear Matt,
Hey, baby, hope you're doing good and killing lots of bad guys. I sent you some beef jerky like you asked and some baby wipes. My mom thought that was

weird, but I explained about how you don't get to shower and all.

I'm gonna have to keep this short because I have to study for bio. Mrs. Crane said we were gonna have a pop quiz, but that was a while ago and I think it might be any day now. I'm sooo scared. I hate bio and I have dreams that the test is today and everybody knows but me and I forgot to study. I try to look off Brad Rigby's paper in the dream and he tells Crane. OMG! I hate bio.

Anyhow, I hope you're good and that you're keeping your gun clean. I saw on TV how the sand gets in them and they don't work. They also said on TV that soldiers like to get tuna fish in those little single-serve packets. Or Crystal Light On the Go packets. Do you want me to send you some?

Love ya,

Caroline

P.S. We beat Briar Cliff last week. This week it's Upper Westfield. Ugh! I hate them!

P.P.S. My little brother did a report on you at school last week. He brought in that old dollar bill you sent from when Saddam was king.

Matt read the letter three times over, culling through it for hidden meanings in every word. Why did she mention

Brad Rigby? And why was she dreaming about him? What did that mean? Everything else suddenly seemed stupid. She was back home and "sooo scared" about a pop quiz in bio while he was in Iraq with some traumatic brain injury.

The normalness of her letters—the bland, ordinary details of high school life—used to make him feel good, like things were the same at home even if he was gone. He'd told himself that that was what he was fighting for: so Caroline and his mom and Lizzy could go to the mall or watch that show they liked, *Gossip Girl*, and do whatever they did and not have to worry.

But now it bugged him that she was suddenly like some expert on the war, telling him to clean his gun and asking if he wanted single-serving packs of tuna. And she'd signed her letter "love ya." That was what she and her girlfriends said when they hung up on their cell phones—or what you say to your mom when you leave the house. What was that supposed to mean?

He looked up from the letter and saw Francis standing next to his bed. He was holding a jar with some kind of cream in his hands.

"'A lightweight lotion that packs all the moisturizing benefits of beta-carotene into a sheer, easily absorbed base,'" he read from the label in a lisping, mock-gay voice. "'The natural way to repair and revive sun-damaged skin.'"

He opened the jar and sniffed. "My kid sister sent it to me," he said. "I told her I needed sunscreen." He shook his head. "Girls. They're like a different species, you know?"

Matt put his hands to his cheeks, an imitation of the *Home Alone* kid. "OMG!" he said in a high, girly voice. "That's what my girlfriend says," he said in a normal voice. "She's like . . . turned into . . . you know . . . that girl, the one who drives her kids around with no seat belt?"

Francis cocked his head to the side. "Britney Spears?"

"Yeah," said Matt. "Her."

"Dude," Francis said. "That brain thing you have. Are you sure you don't have Alzheimer's?"

Matt noticed then that Francis was also holding a picture. "What's that?" he said.

Francis handed him the photo, a picture of a little girl with the same lopsided smile Francis had, standing on a porch all decorated with red, white, and blue streamers. The house looked like it was in a city somewhere, in a not-very-good part of town.

"My kid," Francis said. He stared at the picture for a while. "I told my wife . . ." His voice drifted off. "Have everybody come to the side door. The mailman, the neighbors."

Matt had no idea what he was talking about.

"When the army comes to your door, to give you the bad news," he said, "they always use the front door. The chaplain, the guy with the letter from the president, they come to the front door."

Matt nodded.

"So if everybody we know uses the side door, every time the bell rings, she doesn't have to, you know, imagine the worst."

THE BLOND NURSE, THE ONE WHO LOOKED LIKE BETTY—OR was it Veronica?—had wheeled him to his appointment with Meaghan Finnerty, then left. Matt sat outside the door to her office, studying the things in his notebook.

Kwong had said that Matt might have trouble learning new information. So Matt had written a couple of facts from the World Series trivia book and made a sort of study guide—putting a few of the questions on one side of the page and the answers on the other. Then he folded the page in half, like he used to do when he was studying Spanish vocab, and tested himself.

Which pitcher broke a sixty-two-year-old record when he struck out twenty-nine batters in the 1965 World

Series? What year was the series postponed because of an earthquake? Who holds the series record for most home runs?

He covered the answers with his hand and tried to focus. But as soon as he looked away from the book, his mind went blank.

Meaghan Finnerty opened the door. He was surprised at how glad he was to see her. Then his heart sank: She took out her little deck of flash cards.

But he went along with her, concentrating harder than he ever had in school, struggling to identify pictures of random objects—a radio, a butterfly, a lamp—then trying to fill in the missing words in sentences about situations from what Meaghan Finnerty called everyday life.

"So, if you want to fill up your car and you only have twenty dollars, can you afford eight gallons of regular and still have money left for a Coke?" she asked.

Matt just looked at her. Everyday life wasn't about filling up a gas tank or ordering a bucket of wings. Everyday life was about getting your gas mask on in ten seconds or calibrating the distance between your position and a sniper's nest.

He tried to concentrate. But all the information—the cost of a gallon of gas, the price of a can of Coke—slipped out of his mind as soon as he took his eyes off the page.

His head had begun to ache and his attention had started to drift, when the cry of the muezzin sounded.

The muezzin's call, broadcast from atop a minaret summoning the faithful to prayer, was a regular feature of the Iraqi soundscape. It occurred five times a day, and Matt had long ago gotten used to the strange noise. But this time it felt like it was ringing in his ears, as if the muezzin were standing right next to him. He could see Meaghan's lips moving, but all he could hear were the long, drawn-out strains of the ancient, mournful call. He wiped his hands across his upper lip. He was sweating.

"Are you all right?" Her words reached him as if they were coming from inside a long tunnel.

"Yeah, sure, I'm fine." The last note of the call to prayer lingered in the air for a moment, then stopped. Matt shook his head, trying to get the sound out of his mind, and waited for his breathing to return to normal.

Meaghan Finnerty seemed to be studying him.

"I'm fine, really," he said.

And they went back to the everyday experience of figuring out which was the better buy: medium popcorn and a soda or an extra large and a free soda.

A SKINNY KID WITH PIMPLES DOTTING HIS FOREHEAD WAS waiting for him with a wheelchair outside Meaghan Finnerty's office.

This kid was about his age. He had one earbud stuck in his ear and a dab of zit cream on his neck.

"Okay if I walk?" Matt asked.

"Nope." The kid set the brake on the wheelchair with his foot. He was wearing high-tops. Few of the people in the hospital wore combat boots, Matt had noticed. Most of the doctors wore clogs, although one wore socks with sandals, and the nurses all seemed to wear sneakers. It felt more like a mall than an army hospital sometimes. The pimply kid shrugged. "Doctor says you're not allowed."

Matt sighed and lowered himself into the chair, secretly relieved. He was keeping track of how many steps he'd gone since he'd gotten here—so far, sixty-four was the max—and Meaghan Finnerty's office was actually pretty far from the ward.

He wheeled the chair around a corner, then turned up the volume on his iPod. It was so loud, Matt could hear the clatter of the cymbals. "What are you listening to?" he asked after a while.

"It's kinda old-school," he said. "The Clash. Mood music for Iraq."

Without another word, the kid pulled the other earbud out of the pocket of his scrubs and handed it to Matt. And they went down the hall, tethered to each other, listening to "Rock the Casbah."

Matt and Caroline used to share a pair of earphones like that on the bus on the way home from school. They'd sit in the last row and sometimes Matt would just marvel at the look of her knee next to his. Her legs were pale and lean and her skin was impossibly soft, and when she wore a short skirt to school, it drove him crazy. Sometimes, when the squad was riding in the Humvee, he had to fight the urge to take off his helmet and look at the picture of her in her cheerleading uniform, to look at her legs and imagine the two of them together again, sitting in the back of the bus.

When the song ended, he handed the earbud back.

"You don't have anything, like, seriously wrong with you, do you?" the kid asked.

"No," Matt said. "Other than not being able to remember what a raincoat is."

The kid stopped the wheelchair a minute. "Like any internal bleeding or anything?"

Matt shook his head.

"Good. Because I think I can probably pop a wheelie on this thing if we get up enough speed."

THE CHORUS OF "BORN IN THE USA" CAME FLOATING OUT of the ward as Matt walked in. The soldier with the yo-yo—his name was Clarence, Matt was pretty sure—was fiddling with the dial on a radio that had suddenly appeared on his bedside table.

"107.7 FM. Classic Rock," he said. "Freedom Radio. Courtesy of the U.S. Army."

After the last few chords of the song died out, an announcer with a Southern accent came on and said there would be a Bible study group meeting on Wednesday and confidential evaluations at the combat stress clinic on Thursday. Life in the Green Zone.

But the strangest thing about the Green Zone was the quiet—or rather, the ordinariness of the sounds. Cell phones trilling. Toilets flushing. The hiss of air as someone pulled the tab on a can of Coke. The sounds were both odd and familiar—out of place, ordinary, and extraordinary at the same time. Matt thought about Itchy, the cat, and how he'd grown accustomed to the pounding of mortar fire and wondered if he would stop noticing these everyday sounds and get used to the quiet.

He opened his notebook to the page with the baseball trivia questions and tested himself again. He was pretty sure Sandy Koufax was the guy who held the strike-out record, but he couldn't remember if the World Series was postponed because an earthquake in 1989 or 1998. He unfolded the page. It was 1989. He repeated that to himself: 1989, 1989, 1989. He tested himself again. But he couldn't remember. Was it '89? Or '98?

A warm breeze filtered in through the open window, carrying the crackle of static, then the lulling voice of an Iraqi sports announcer narrating a soccer match. Soon, Matt felt fatigue descend on him. He closed his eyes and let the notebook slide from his grasp.

Then he heard gunshots. The staccato *pop-pop-pop* of an AK-47.

Matt bolted upright, clutching the covers in his fists. The popping grew louder, closer; the shots seemed to be coming from every direction.

He didn't have his gun or his helmet. He didn't have his vest and he wasn't wearing his boots. He was in a hospital bed, wearing nothing but a pair of shorts and flip-flops.

For a moment everything went quiet. A single shot rang out, ricocheting off the concrete.

And suddenly Matt was back in the alley. In the distance, he could see a little boy, ducking in and out of a doorway. A candy wrapper fluttered from a coil of razor wire. The quivering radio voice of a woman singing a love song floated through the air. Machine-gun fire erupted. Bits of plaster rained down from overhead. A dog, a mangy stray with a crooked tail, trotted across the street, oblivious to the battle around him. A single shot rang out. The child was lifted into the air, paddling his arms like a swimmer. He looked surprised, then confused, then absolutely terrified as he soared through the turquoise sky, higher and higher, until all Matt could see were the soles of his shoes.

Matt opened his eyes. All he could see was the deep green of the army blanket. He flushed with embarrassment. He had pulled the covers over his head like a baby.

His whole body was shaking violently. He listened for a moment. The ward was hushed, the only sounds were the steady beeping of a medical monitor a few beds away and the distant rush of water from a toilet flushing.

Slowly, carefully, he pulled the blanket away from his eyes. He heard a voice from a few rows away. It was the shop teacher with the bad back. "Dumb hajis," he said. "Shooting off their machine guns just because they won a soccer game."

Matt looked around. He saw the guy with the yo-yo showing a nurse one of his tricks. Francis was scribbling in his notebook, and the two guys at the end of the room were playing cards. No one had even looked in his direction.

Matt wrapped the blanket around his fist, put it to his mouth, and sobbed.

MATT WAS WAITING OUTSIDE MEAGHAN FINNERTY'S OFFICE in the hallway when she arrived for work early the next morning. The sun wasn't even up yet, and the hospital was shrouded in the silence that descended on it only rarely, in those predawn hours after the last of the night's casualties were taken care of and the day's new patients had yet to arrive.

She stiffened, unconsciously bringing her hand to her service revolver as she saw him sitting in the darkened hallway.

"One hundred and three," he said. "There are one hundred and three steps between here and the ward."

She scowled, but she eased her hand away from her holster.

Matt held up the notebook that Francis had given him. "I know for sure," he said. "I wrote it down."

She turned her wrist to check her watch. It wasn't even seven in the morning. He had no business being off the ward, and she could report him if she wanted to.

"Can we do some more of those picture cards today?" he said quickly. "Ma'am?"

"At our appointment," she said. "This afternoon."

Matt stuffed his hands in his pockets and went to leave. He took a step, then turned to face her. "You're, like, the guidance counselor here, right?"

"Not really," she said.

"But if a person has something they need to talk about, they can talk to you?"

"You can talk to Father Brennan," she said.

"It's not a religion thing. It's a memory thing."

Meaghan Finnerty cocked her head to the side and studied him. In her gaze, he saw a flicker of sympathy, something he hadn't sensed from her before, and he looked away, out the window, so she couldn't see the tears that had suddenly welled up in his eyes.

It was still sort of dark out; all he could make out in the dim, gauzy light was the silhouette of a palm tree. He counted to ten to try to regain his composure before turning to leave.

"Come in," she said.

"Something bad happened," he said. In the stillness of the early morning, the tiny room felt deserted, hushed, like a church before Mass. "Something really bad."

She nodded.

"I keep seeing it in my head. Or parts of it, anyhow." He wiped his hands on his pant legs, not looking up.

"That's not unusual," she said. "A lot of soldiers have flashbacks, disturbing memories, nightmares. . . ."

"It doesn't make sense," he said, his voice cracking. "I keep seeing him."

"Who?"

"This street kid," Matt said, toying with his plastic hospital wristband.

She waited.

"His parents were killed and he lives with his sister. Inside a giant drainage pipe. One of those things we brought over to rebuild the place. Except we never did."

He paused.

"He's a really good artist. And he runs circles around us on the soccer field. He can score a goal from twenty yards out." Matt glanced up at her for a moment. "He's like Itchy, this cat we adopted. Like our mascot."

Meaghan Finnerty furrowed her brow. "I don't understand."

Matt hung his head. "Me neither."

The room was absolutely still. Matt could hear the hands on the wall clock advancing, second by second.

He took a deep breath, then spoke so quietly, he wasn't sure he'd said it out loud. "I think I killed him."

MEAGHAN FINNERTY DIDN'T BLINK. SHE JUST LEANED forward in her chair, and a slender beam of light snuck out from underneath the shade behind her.

Matt looked away, at the exit sign above her door, its Arabic and English letters glowing red in the weak morning light.

"He's . . . I . . . he's one of those kids who's always hanging around, asking for candy. He's so skinny . . ." Matt's voice trailed off.

He stopped and gazed out the window for a moment. It was oddly quiet, still, as if the whole city were asleep. He took in the sight of Meaghan Finnerty studying him.

"I was in this alley . . ." he said finally. "I was crouched behind a car, taking fire. And there was this dog. He trots across the street. In the middle of a fucking firefight."

71

He paused, then shook his head. "Up at the other end of the alley, I see this kid ducking in and out of a doorway. And . . ."

The *ping* of the elevator bell drifted in from the hallway. Then came the clatter of metal wheels and the aroma of bacon—an orderly bringing the breakfast cart—and then the deep-timbred laughter of a pair of male voices right outside the door. The loudspeaker crackled and a voice came on reading the day's announcements, including a lecture at 1800 hours on the importance of proper hydration. The hospital was coming, suddenly and loudly, to life. And whatever feeling of intimacy there'd been in the hushed, predawn hallway vanished.

"After that . . ." Matt sighed. "I don't really know what happened."

MATT HAD ONLY GONE A FEW DOZEN YARDS FROM MEAGHAN Finnerty's office when he had to stop and sit down. He saw a chair outside another office and sunk heavily into it.

He was exhausted, having been up half the night, replaying the scene from the alley in his head, but he was also wound up, jumpy, the way Francis was after he'd

72

taken a couple capsules of Ripped Fuel.

Meaghan Finnerty had said she'd work on helping Matt remember more about the incident—she called it that, too, just like Kwong had—at their afternoon appointment.

But Matt couldn't wait. He pulled the notebook out of his pocket and looked at the puppies on the front cover, tumbling over one another. He flipped past the page of baseball trivia and turned to a fresh page. "The Incident," he labeled it. He numbered each entry and wrote down what happened just the way Justin had described it.

1. *taxi runs the southern checkpoint*
2. *Justin and I pursue the vehicle*
3. *we turn down a side road, past the bootleg store*
4. *we get out of the Humvee to give chase down an alley*
5. *we take fire*
6. *we go into a house*
7. *Justin picks off the shooter from an upstairs window*
8. *we leave the building, RPG hits wall*

Matt looked at his careful, precise handwriting. In high school his writing was so sloppy, he could hardly read it himself sometimes. But after his drill sergeant had yelled at him, saying unreadable coordinates on a battle-field could cost lives—Matt had taught himself to print according to SOP. Standard operating procedure.

SOP. It was also standard operating procedure to keep the squad together, to always have the other guys in sight if possible. If not in sight, at least in touch by radio. But McNally and Wolf and the others weren't there during the chase. Justin said they'd gotten separated.

Matt closed his eyes. And saw the dog again. It was weird the way it trotted across the alley, right in the middle of the firefight. Matt couldn't get it out of his mind. But Justin hadn't seen the dog. Which didn't make sense.

Unless Matt had been alone in the alley.

THE CAFETERIA HAD A GREASY, FAST-FOOD SMELL, A HUMID, tropical climate all its own. Matt walked in slowly, edging his way along the wall, watching people swarm by. It was his first attempt to venture into the mess hall since Dr. Kwong had given him permission to leave the ward for meals.

"Your X-rays came back fine. No skull fracture.

No neck or spinal instability," the doctor had said. "Have any vomiting? Any dizziness? Problems with coordination? Any, uh, emotional agitation or any other, uh, problems?"

Matt's right leg was still weak and out of sync with his left, and he still found himself on the verge of tears half the time. "Nope," he said. "I'm all good."

"Well, that's what they like to hear," he'd said.

"Who?" Matt said. "Who likes to hear?"

"CPA."

There were so many initials in the army. IED, MRE, RPG. It took him a minute to remember what CPA was. Central Provisional Authority.

"They like us to get you fellas patched up and back out there as soon as possible," Kwong had said. "A young, healthy kid like you ought to be back with your unit in a couple of days."

There was a slight hint of sarcasm in Kwong's voice, and Matt wondered if Kwong was under pressure to get soldiers back in the field more quickly than he would like. But all Matt really heard was the part about rejoining his unit soon.

"Meanwhile," Kwong had said, "let's see if we can't bulk you up a little."

The sour aroma of overcooked coffee drifted by, and a pair of officers in neatly pressed pants appeared, carrying trays of steaming food. There were a handful of men in uniform, but almost everyone in the room was dressed in scrubs. Matt felt foolish in his T-shirt, shorts, and flip-flops, almost as naked as if he were in a hospital gown. But he took a deep breath and stepped away from the wall, aware that his right leg was dragging, and he felt himself be pulled into the tide of people heading toward the chow line.

He shuffled through the line mechanically and watched as men in white knit Muslim skullcaps doled out eggs and bacon with stoic, expressionless faces. Then he found himself suddenly back out among the chairs and tables, holding a heaping tray of food. Matt felt his knees begin to give out and he sat down abruptly at the nearest table.

The guy next to him, a burly man with a faux-hawk, poured ketchup onto his grits and talked loudly in Spanish to another soldier across the table. The only words Matt could make out were "Paris Hilton."

He looked down at the grease around his eggs congealing on his plate and pushed his hash browns around with a fork. He pictured Ali going up to take Communion, his brown, bloated belly and the way he gobbled up the Host. He shoved his tray away, then got up and allowed himself to be pulled into the tide of people bringing their plates to the dish room.

ON HIS WAY BACK TO THE WARD HE SAW AN ORDERLY COMING toward him, pushing a gurney. There was no patient on the cart but, rather, something oddly familiar, something large and black, plastic and weirdly lumpy. A body bag.

Matt stopped, stood at attention, his eyes locked onto an imaginary point on the wall as he approached.

He meant to hold his gaze steady, at a respectful distance from the body bag itself, but something about it caught his eye. It was, it seemed, strangely deflated. Instead of the unmistakable outline of a corpse, which was usually visible through the plastic, only one end of the bag seemed full.

Matt thought back to the attack that had killed Sergeant Benson, their first squad leader. His leg had been blown off at the knee, and so it had to be placed in the body bag separately. But still, they'd taken pains to lay his body out in its proper configuration. He'd heard of guys being so badly blown up that all that was left of them were body parts, and he felt his stomach roil at the thought that perhaps that was what was inside the bag as it drew near.

Still, he kept his head erect, his back stiff, his mouth set in a straight line as the gurney got closer. Then, just as it passed by, he flinched.

MATT SPOTTED THE PIMPLY-FACED KID RESTOCKING A SUPPLY closet as he came down the hall toward his ward. His name was Pete. Matt had written it in his notebook. It was the only entry on the page "Things I Know."

"Dude," Matt said, "can I bum a smoke off you?"

"Only if I can come with you," Pete said. "If anyone asks, you say you were feeling weak and you needed me, you know, to get a wheelchair or a bedpan or something."

"A bedpan?" Matt said.

Pete shrugged. "You want me to say you needed an enema?"

Matt got the joke. Meaghan Finnerty had said he might have trouble with "social cues," but this was the second time he'd understood when someone was trying to be funny. A good sign.

The two of them stepped outside, into an inferno. The sudden heat—as startling as a grenade blast—nearly knocked him back. It was the first time Matt had been outside in . . . he quickly calculated . . . three days or so, and already he'd forgotten the way Iraq could cook a man alive.

The two of them sat on a stone wall while Pete pulled a pack of cigarettes out of the pocket of his scrubs. He lit one for himself, then handed the pack to Matt.

Matt lit a cigarette, inhaled deeply, then coughed up a plume of smoke.

"Been a while," he said to Pete when he'd caught his breath. The truth was that he had never been a very good smoker; he could never quite hit the right balance between inhaling too much or too little. But smoking was one of those things he picked up, or at least tried to pick up, when the squad had any downtime.

He'd even bought a carton of Marlboros when they left Kuwait for Baghdad, but he'd lost most of them the first night they got to Sadr City. While Matt was outside waiting in line for the latrine, Wolf and Justin took all his stuff—his bedroll, his night-vision goggles, his DVD player, his stash of beef jerky—and divvied it up among the other guys. When he got back from the latrine, all that was left was his cot.

Matt had been forced to "buy" all his gear back, paying with the cigarettes he'd hidden in his duffel. After that, whenever he wanted to smoke, he had to bum his own cigarettes off the guys. Wolf, who was only a couple years older than Matt, always asked him to show ID.

Pete exhaled, then said out of nowhere, "You think

your whole life flashes before your eyes when you die, like they say?"

Matt had thought about this before. He couldn't fathom how eighteen years of Christmas mornings and riding bikes and playing war with Lizzy could flash before your eyes. Was it a sudden flash, he wondered, like a bomb blast—where your whole life explodes in your mind's eye? Or was it like a home movie—with jerky images going by in fast-forward one last time?

"I don't know," he said.

"What if the last thing you see is something awful, like, you know . . ." His voice trailed off. "Or what if it's something stupid? Like a chicken feather?"

Matt just looked at him. "A chicken feather?"

"This one guy, this Iraqi guy, was riding his bike home from the market with a chicken tied to his handlebar," Pete said. "Got blown up by an IED. He had feathers all over him when they brought him in. He didn't remember a thing about the explosion. All he cared about was his chicken."

Matt could picture the whole scene. The flying debris. The fine gray ash that settles over everything afterward. He could even imagine one single chicken feather floating back down to earth, cartoon-style, and the man lying in the rubble, dazed.

"Why do you think that happens?" Matt asked.

"Why do chickens get killed in wars?" Pete said. "You're not, like, a vegetarian or something, are you?"

This time, the joke was lost on Matt. He was too deep in thought. "The explosion," Matt said. "Why couldn't he remember it?"

Pete shrugged. "Too much for the brain to handle, I guess," he said.

"I keep remembering things . . ." Matt said.

Pete ground his cigarette out under the toe of his high-tops. "Dude," he said, "sometimes it's better not to remember."

"SMALL TOWN" WAS PLAYING ON FREEDOM RADIO WHEN Matt walked onto the ward. He took in the faintly stale smell of men's bodies and felt a pang of something that he could only describe as homesickness. Homesickness for his squad. For the guys. Maybe it had to do with seeing the body bag. He didn't just miss the guys. He was worried about how they were doing without him. He was the only guy who really knew how to fix the MK-19 on their Humvee when it got jammed.

Matt wandered up to the nurses' station, where Francis was talking to Nurse McCrae. "I'll trade you a carton of Marlboro Lights, a twenty-dollar phone card, and I'll throw in a *Grey's Anatomy*. Third season. Please," he said, taking hold of her wrist. "Just a couple tabs. So I can sleep."

Nurse McCrae freed her hand from his grasp, then tied and untied a piece of yarn around her pigtail. "Sergeant," she said, sighing, "I do not need to get in trouble over this. And neither do you."

Then she walked away, leaving Francis at the desk, cursing under his breath. Matt put a hand on his shoulder. Francis spun around and took a wild swing, nearly hitting Matt in the jaw.

"Jesus Christ!" Francis said. "Why'd you sneak up on me like that?"

Matt took a few steps back, his hands in the air as if he were surrendering. "Whoa, dude, easy."

But Francis leaned in even closer, so close that Matt could smell the coffee on his breath.

"You afraid of me?" he said.

Matt shrugged. There was no right answer to that question.

"Well, you should be." Francis's eyes were locked on Matt's. "Because I killed my squad leader."

Matt felt his stomach drop.

"You wanted to know why I'm here," Francis said. "Now you know. You wanna know the rest?"

Matt nodded almost imperceptibly. He didn't want to know. But he knew Francis had to tell him.

"One night, our piece of shit Humvee breaks down on a dinner run and so our convoy stops, like sitting ducks," he said. "Out of nowhere we get hit by an RPG. Half of us run right, half go left. But it's dark, like twilight, and we can't find each other because our radios are fucked up."

Francis looked off in the middle distance and Matt knew he was seeing the whole thing all over again.

"All you can see is shapes, silhouettes. And I turn a corner and see a muzzle flash. Thirty yards away. And I just laser in on it and fire. I see an arm pop up, waving side to side, like the guy is saying hello. Then he goes down. After the smoke clears, I go over and take a look. And it's my squad leader."

Matt felt his knees actually go weak.

Francis went on. "But now I hear from a buddy of mine back in Kuwait that the radio fuckup was because we didn't have the right fucking encryption codes. Some douchebag changed them and forgot to tell us.

"I'm here in the loony bin," Francis said. "And that douchebag is still out there."

Matt blinked. He looked down the row of beds. No one, he realized, had any serious injuries, except maybe Clarence, but he was a nut job in a Rambo kind of way.

He thought back to his first night in the hospital and pictured the kid with the missing hand. The next day, the kid was gone. Or was *he* the one who was gone? To some kind of special ward?

"You know what happened to the douche who sent us out there with the wrong codes? He got demoted." Francis paused for a second. "You know what the penalty is for killing a civilian here?"

Matt swallowed.

"Twenty years," Francis said. "Twenty years for killing a haji and a demotion for getting my buddy killed!" He reached under his pillow and pulled out his notebook. He waved it in the air. "Well, I've got it all right here."

But Matt wasn't listening any longer. Twenty years. He'd be thirty-eight by then.

"You said last time that you were in an alley. . . ." Meaghan Finnerty said as she closed her door.

She was acting like they'd just pick up where they'd left off. Matt thought maybe they'd ease into the conversation, talk about the weather or something first.

He nodded.

"You were under fire. . . ." She was waiting for him to continue.

But Matt didn't like how fast this was going. He needed to explain. About how he could remember some parts and not others.

"Can a person do something and not remember it?" he asked abruptly.

Meaghan Finnerty leaned back in her chair. "I suppose . . ." she said. "There are some soldiers who experience posttraumatic amnesia. It's common with head injuries."

Matt unconsciously lifted his hand to his head, to the tender spot at the base of his skull.

She went on. "There are two kinds of amnesia," she said. "Anterograde is when you can't remember what happened after the incident. Retrograde is when you can't remember what happened before."

Matt took his notebook out of his back pocket. He asked her to repeat both definitions a few times so he could write them down. *Antero = can't remember what happened after,* he wrote. *Retro = before.*

"I think I mainly have the first one," he said, checking his notebook to be sure. "Where you can't remember what happened before."

She opened the file on her lap.

Matt gripped the arm of his chair. "Are you going to write down everything I say? I thought you said this"—he gestured around the tiny office—"that this was confidential."

She closed the file. "This is the army," she said. "My job is to make an evaluation about your fitness to return to duty."

Matt felt sick. All he could think of was what Francis had said about the jail term for killing a civilian. An image of his mother came into his head, his mother pressing a Kleenex to her lips and trying not to cry. His mother and his little sister, Lizzy, in a courtroom, huddled together on a bench.

"Matt," Meaghan Finnerty said.

It registered, dimly, that she had never called him by name before. He was always "Private Duffy" or "soldier." He just looked at her. She really was pretty, in a pale, delicate kind of way; she probably only weighed a hundred pounds. And she was going to be the one who got him court-martialed.

"Matt," she said again, as if she were scolding him.

He worked very hard now to pay attention, to stop thinking about how he would tell his mom.

"I hear a lot of things in this office," she said carefully. "And I *forget* a lot of what I hear. Do you understand what I'm saying?"

He nodded. But he didn't understand. And then, all at once, he did.

This is the army, she had said. This was classic army behavior: to ignore certain breaches of the code. To say,

"Sir, no, sir, I did not see Private Duffy giving his ration to that little boy," as Justin had done when Matt gave his freeze-dried package of mac and cheese to Ali once. "I didn't see a thing, sir."

"My job is to do evaluations," Meaghan Finnerty said. "No more. No less. I can try to help you remember what you want to remember." She paused. "But I don't have to put it in my report."

Matt was too stunned to even nod.

"But make no mistake, Private Duffy," she said. "I will not send a soldier back to duty if I don't judge him to be ready. I will not send a man into combat if I believe that he is, in any way, a danger to himself, to his fellow soldiers, or to the Iraqi people."

He nodded this time, reflexively.

"Do we understand each other?" she said, tucking her hair behind her ear.

"Yes, ma'am," he said.

They both sat there a while, listening to the hum of hospital life outside her tiny office. From the distance came the sound of an approaching helicopter. The sound became a roar as the medevac landed on the roof. Eventually the engine wound down and the blades stopped churning. Finally Meaghan Finnerty leaned forward.

"So . . ." she began again. "You were in an alley. . . ."

He nodded.

"You were under fire." She paused.

"Uh-huh," Matt said.

"And you mentioned a dog. . . ."

"That's one of the things that doesn't add up," Matt said. "Justin, my buddy, the guy who saved me, saved my life, he didn't see the dog."

She furrowed her brow. "This was during the same incident? Is it possible you're confusing two separate events?"

"No. I'm sure," he said. He stopped for a minute. "I remember sparks, too. Bullets kicking up sparks on the street. Right in front of the dog. He was sniffing through the trash. He didn't even move."

She looked a little dubious.

"It happens," he said. "The animals here get used to it. Our cat, Itchy. If there's shelling, he sleeps right through it."

"No," she said. "I don't doubt that. I just . . ." She tapped her pen against the file. "Can you think of any reason why Justin wouldn't have seen what you saw?"

Matt nodded. Then he shook his head. "But he wouldn't do that," Matt said, more to himself than to Meaghan Finnerty. He blinked, then looked up at her. "He wouldn't have left me in that alley by myself."

"But that's how you remember it?" she said. "That

88

you were there alone."

"Yes, ma'am."

"Well, sometimes," she said, "the memories that don't make sense are the ones you have to pay attention to."

Matt tried to take this in. There were so many things that didn't make sense.

"The little boy . . ." she said. "You mentioned a little boy last time. He was at the other end of the alley."

Matt nodded.

"Was it the little boy you told me about? The one who was like your mascot?"

Matt closed his eyes and saw it all again. The flash of light, the strange expression on Ali's face, his arms thrashing.

Suddenly, the office door shook, as startling as a burst of machine-gun fire.

Matt jumped to his feet.

A male voice from the other side called out Meaghan's name. "I'll be right with you," she said. Then to Matt, "My next appointment."

He nodded, his heart still pounding.

"Don't worry," she said. "A lot of guys jump when they hear a door slam or a car backfire," she said. "Normal sounds can trigger the body to go into its fight-or-flight mode. Once you've been in combat, you're wired to be on the lookout for threats."

Matt knew what she meant. Itchy might be able to ignore the sounds of combat, but at the slightest sound the guys in his squad would wake up out of a sound sleep, jump out of bed, and pull their gear on. Wolf once put his gas mask on in the middle of a dream. And one time Figueroa hit the ground in the middle of the street when the wind knocked down a wooden sign.

"Just keep track of everything in your notebook," Meaghan said. "Random memories. Noises, sights that trigger you."

"Okay," he said. "Ma'am. Thank you, ma'am."

"But Private," she said as he turned to leave, "I'd keep that notebook on the DL."

"So, Private, are you enjoying your stay here?" Dr. Kwong asked, glancing up from Matt's chart. "The nurses tell me you're getting stronger every day."

"Yes, sir," Matt said. "Sir? This thing I have—TBI. How do I know when I'm better?"

Kwong hung the clipboard at the foot of the bed and pulled a tiny penlight from his pocket. "There's no clear scientific way, if that's what you mean." He came around to the head of the bed and shined the light in Matt's eye.

"It's more the absence of indicators—you understand?"

Matt nodded. But he wasn't sure he really did grasp what the doctor was saying.

"You still having language-retrieval problems?" Kwong said.

"Some."

"Mood swings?" Kwong's voice came from over Matt's shoulder as he shined his light in Matt's ears.

Matt blinked. "Sort of."

"How about your cognitive functioning? Are you able to absorb new information?" Kwong had put on his stethoscope and was listening to Matt's heart. If Matt answered, what would it sound like through the stethoscope? Would his voice rumble in Kwong's ears? Or would it sound like a fly buzzing just out of range?

"How about focus?" Kwong asked, his stethoscope now on Matt's back. "Are you having trouble concentrating?"

Matt tried to think. He couldn't even remember what Kwong's last question was.

"Not really," he said.

The doctor took off his stethoscope and stood in front of Matt. "Now let me see you take a few steps."

Matt slid off the bed and walked over to the window, exaggerating his posture and working hard to take even, measured steps so Kwong wouldn't notice the way his right leg dragged ever so slightly. When he turned around to come back, Kwong was making notes.

"One day, you'll notice that the fuzziness is gone," he said. "Then you'll know you're better."

PETE SHOWED UP AT THE NURSES' STATION A LITTLE WHILE later, a pillowcase slung over his shoulder. He looked like a skinny, underage Santa in scrubs. He scanned the ward, spotted Matt, and came over.

"A care package," he said, setting the pillowcase on Matt's bed. He reached in and pulled out a box of Little Debbies. "Oatmeal Cream Pie," he said. "Not the best, but better than the Zebra Crunch."

Matt sighed. A bunch of second-graders had sent his squad a mother lode of Little Debbies. Little Debbie must have gotten herself on some kind of list for what to send to soldiers.

Pete reached into the pillowcase again. "A slightly used copy of *Chicken Soup for the Cat Lover's Soul: Stories of Feline Affection, Mystery and Charm*."

"Where do you get this stuff?" Matt said.

Pete shrugged his skinny shoulders. "Around."

"You're not, like, taking stuff from . . . you know,

where they keep supplies. . . ."

Pete held up his hand. "'Don't ask, don't tell,'" he said. He started to walk away. "Oh," he called out over his shoulder, loud enough for everyone to hear, "I also threw in a copy of that *Us Weekly* you asked for. The one with Zac Efron on the cover."

THERE WERE A COUPLE OF MPS WAITING AT THE NURSES' station when Matt got back from lunch. He tried to pick up his pace as he went past, but his right leg was still weak and dragging a bit, which meant he sort of half hopped as he went by.

"Is this the soldier?" one of them said. He was a skinny guy with a skinny mustache.

The blond nurse nodded, and Matt's mouth went dry.

"Private Duffy?" the other one said. "We'd like you to come with us." He was a beefy guy, Hispanic-looking, and he held his arms rigidly at his sides.

Matt swallowed. "Where?" was all he could say.

"With us," the skinny one said. Then he extended his arm out toward Matt at an angle that made it look like he was offering to walk him down a wedding aisle.

Matt didn't know if he was supposed to take the guy's arm or what, so he shoved his hands in his pockets.

"Lieutenant Colonel Fuchs's office," the beefy one said. "They have some questions for you."

Matt glanced over toward Francis's bed. It was empty. Maybe Francis was in trouble for his black-market business. Maybe that was what this was about.

A sickening sensation in his gut told him otherwise. He felt for his notebook in his back pocket. "Okay," he said.

THE MPs ESCORTED MATT THROUGH THE HOSPITAL, DOWN to a lobby of some kind where there was a giant mural of Saddam that someone had tried to cover with an American flag, and then held the door open and led him outside. A ferocious gust of hot air blew in, and Matt had to struggle to push his way through it.

As they stepped out into the sudden sunlight, his eyes went weak and achy; for a minute he was unable to see where he was going.

The skinny one kept his hand on Matt's shoulder as they crossed some kind of courtyard that seemed to be full of Americans in khaki pants walking purposefully this way and that. The two MPs mainly ignored him, grousing about their mosquito bites and debating whether cigar smoke kept the bugs away at night.

After a little while, the skinny one let go of his shoulder and Matt found himself trailing along behind them. He couldn't be the one in trouble, he told himself, or they'd keep him firmly between them, constantly in their sights the way soldiers on patrol did when they took an Iraqi into custody.

A moment later, they stepped inside what seemed like a large, ornate building, and Matt found himself barely able to see in the sudden dark. After his eyes adjusted, he saw that the halls were made of marble and the walls adorned with Arabic words in fancy gold lettering.

"Used to be Saddam's palace," one of them, the beefy one, said to Matt.

Another good sign. They wouldn't be so friendly if he was in trouble.

A moment later, he heard the percussive thump of hip-hop coming from a boom box. They rounded a corner and he found himself inside a vast room of some kind, where soldiers were painting a mural of the Twin Towers on the wall. One soldier was holding a bag of Doritos as he worked.

The room, which was practically as big as a football field, had marble floors, marble walls, a balcony around the top, and a gigantic crystal chandelier. In the middle of the floor were rows of metal-frame canvas cots, each one topped with mosquito netting; around the edge of the room were a dozen Porta Potties. The whole place looked like some kind of weird, palatial summer camp. As Matt and the MPs walked by, the soldier holding the bag of Doritos looked over at Matt and gave him a wry, better-you-than-me look.

Finally they crossed through a giant rotunda with a turquoise dome and came to a hallway with a long row of heavy doors. The skinny one pointed to an ornate wrought-iron bench and told Matt to sit down and wait until someone came for him. Then they left.

MATT COULD HEAR THE RUMBLE OF MALE VOICES FROM THE other side of the door but couldn't make out what anyone was saying. His knee was bouncing up and down and his heart was pounding the way it used to when it was his turn in Public Speaking class.

A few minutes later, the door behind him opened and out walked a pair of Iraqi men, each of them wearing a long, flowing tunic, the Iraqi clothing Justin called a "mandress." They were grumbling and talking to each other and hardly noticed Matt.

"Hello," he said in Arabic. *"Al Salaam a'alaykum."* It was a reflex, a habit from months of street patrols. He'd nearly flunked Spanish sophomore year, but Matt had picked up a good bit of Arabic, a skill that had helped defuse more than one tense situation. Even Charlene had had to grudgingly ask for his help when she wanted to buy a scarf at the bazaar.

The elder of the men—the one wearing a Western jacket over his mandress—stopped, bowed, and greeted Matt in return.

Then the men left. He could still make out the sound of voices from behind the door, but the tenor was different, lighter, more conversational. Then, plain as day, came the sound of a television. The door opened and a first lieutenant, a balding, thickset man, stepped out. Lieutenant Brody, according to his name tag.

"Private Duffy?" he said.

Matt jumped to his feet and saluted.

"At ease, soldier," he said. "Please come in."

Matt noticed two things about the room the minute he stepped inside: a TV showing a college basketball game and an officer, a lieutenant colonel with a regulation crew cut, seated behind a large wooden desk. It was the officer who'd given Matt his Purple Heart, Lieutenant Colonel Fuchs. Matt stood at attention and saluted.

"Private Duffy," Fuchs said, getting up from behind his desk and walking across a thick Persian carpet. "Last time I saw you, son, you didn't look so hot."

"Yes, sir," Matt said, still holding his salute. "No, sir, I mean. I didn't." He didn't look so hot right now, either, Matt thought, standing there in his shorts and flip-flops.

"Well, son, it is my great pleasure to meet you, to see you looking like a soldier again and to thank you for your service." He extended his hand.

No one had said anything in basic training about what to do when an officer wants to shake your hand. But Matt lowered his salute and offered his hand in return, slowly becoming aware that it was part of the unspoken code of the army. Normally a guy this high-ranking would treat him like he was invisible. But if you were injured, you were a hero. Matt knew it was supposed to make him feel good, but it just made him more nervous.

"You're welcome, sir," Matt said.

The room was quiet except for the hushed tone of the sportscaster narrating the game, and Matt found he had to make a real effort not to look at the basketball game on the screen behind Lieutenant Colonel Fuchs, where a point guard with cornrows was walking the ball up the court.

"Son," Fuchs said, turning to face the screen, "I want you to watch this boy. Number twelve. He has one hell of a jump shot."

The three of them stood there—in Saddam Hussein's old palace, watching a kid in the United States take a jump shot. This, Matt thought, was a war story no one would believe.

"Blast!" Fuchs said, when the ball bounced off the rim. Then he walked over to the TV and switched the channel to FOX News. "Well, everyone's allowed to fuck up once," he said, gesturing to an upholstered chair in front of the desk. "Take a load off, Private."

Matt eased himself into a stiff upholstered chair.

"So, Private Duffy," the balding one, Brody, was talking now. "They've got you under observation. TBI, is that correct?"

"Yes, sir," Matt said, focusing his gaze on a spot in the middle distance: SOP when dealing with a senior officer.

"Son," Fuchs said, "you can relax. You're among friends here."

"Yes, sir," Matt said, still rigid in his seat.

"At ease, Private," said Fuchs. "And that's an order."

"Okay." Matt shifted a bit in an effort to look relaxed, but he ended up in an awkward rearrangement of his limbs that made him feel even more uncomfortable. "Sir."

Brody cleared his throat. "Private, as we said, we're

happy to see you making a full recovery and expect you'll be as pleased as we will be to get you back into uniform."

Matt looked down at his flip-flops. "Yes, sir," he said. "I . . . uh . . . miss my buddies, sir."

"Good," he said. "We just have one matter to deal with first." He picked up a file folder from the edge of the desk. "A bit of unpleasantness with the locals," he said. "You understand?"

Matt swallowed.

"Good," he said again, as if Matt had said yes. "They've made some claims about a recent incident."

Matt's head was pounding and he could feel his lunch churning in his gut.

"They claim that one of the casualties, a child, was killed intentionally." He opened the folder. "Ayyad Mahmud Aladdin Kimadi is the name."

Matt went numb. It was like the time his squad's convoy was hit by an IED. He'd seen a bright flash up ahead, then a cloud of dust. He actually felt the Humvee go up in the air and come back down. The force of the blast blew his door into the bushes, but Matt just unbuckled his seat belt, walked away, and started firing.

"Ali." Matt's voice cracked as he said the boy's name.

The two senior officers studied him intently.

When Ali had first told him his full, mile-long

name, Matt replied, in slow, halting Arabic, "I'm going to call you Ali." And Ali had thumped his skinny chest with his fist and replied with his favorite bit of English slang: "Word."

Fuchs coughed. "You knew the boy?" he said.

Matt struggled to regain his composure. He cleared his throat, coughed, cleared his throat again. "Yes, sir."

The other officer, Brody, went on as if Matt hadn't said a thing. "We had the body brought up from the morgue here when they called the incident to our attention," he said. "No one had come to claim it."

"His sister," Matt said. "They live in . . . They're homeless."

"Well, of course, we've given the . . . tribal elders the standard death gratuity."

Matt had heard about the death gratuity; it was about the equivalent of 2,500 U.S. dollars.

Brody went on. "And our condolences, of course."

He kept saying "of course," as if this were routine procedure. And somehow Matt found himself nodding as if it were routine to him, too. As if they were acting out lines from a TV show. The actual TV, the one behind Lieutenant Colonel Fuchs, was showing a clip of a soldier in Iraq patrolling a street in Baghdad. It was surreal, Matt thought, and he forced himself to look away, to pay attention to what Brody was saying.

". . . an investigation, then we'll write up a report." He seemed to have finished speaking.

Matt wiped his palms on his shorts. "I, uh . . ." He swallowed. "I . . ."

It would be a relief, somehow, to admit it. To explain about the flashbacks and the memory lapses. To confess the whole thing.

"Now, son," Fuchs said, getting up from his desk and turning off the TV behind him. "You don't have to say anything in here. You don't want to say something you might rethink later."

Rethink? What did that mean?

"There's a lot of chaos out there, a lot of confusion about who exactly the enemy is," Fuchs said, sitting back down behind his desk. "They hide behind civilians and they use civilians. There are kids out there throwing grenades, old men burying IEDs." He shook his head and went on.

"Hell," he said. "There was a woman with a baby signaling to some insurgents up on the roof with a grenade launcher. So the squad leader gives the order to take her out." He sighed. "We couldn't even tell if it was a baby or a sack of potatoes she was holding, because another woman came out and grabbed it when the first one got hit."

Matt studied the officer's face. It was deeply tanned

and wrinkled, and despite his neatly trimmed hair, he had bushy gray Santa Claus eyebrows. He was probably someone's father, Matt thought.

"You just can't be sure," Fuchs said slowly, with gravity. "Do you know what I'm saying, son?"

Matt looked directly into his eyes. "Yes, sir," he said.

It was the briefest and most routine of replies, the kind of thing a soldier says a hundred times a day. But Matt hoped that Fuchs could hear in it what he was trying to convey: that he wasn't sure. About anything. He wasn't even sure he understood what Fuchs was saying. Was he telling him to lie?

"Good," said Brody. "Glad to hear it."

Fuchs tapped the file on the corner of his desk. "You take some time to think this over," he said. "When you're feeling a little stronger, Lieutenant Brody will want to ask you some questions." He tipped his chin in Brody's direction. Then he glanced at his watch, picked up an already neat sheaf of papers sitting on his desk, and stacked them even more neatly into shape.

The signal to leave. Matt stood up and saluted. Fuchs nodded. He didn't offer a handshake this time. And the next thing Matt knew, he was back outside in the hallway.

MATT WALKED MECHANICALLY IN THE DIRECTION FROM which he'd come. Then stopped at the juncture of two hallways. His head was killing him and he had no idea which way to go. There were signs in Arabic but no English subtitles and his sense of direction utterly failed him. He looked for landmarks—a potted plant, a clock, something he'd passed on the way to Fuchs's office—but he saw nothing except miles of thickly veined marble stretching in either direction.

He turned right, walked for a while, then stopped, turned around and went back the way he'd come. When he got to the intersection of the hallway that Fuchs's office was on, he stopped again, then decided to continue down that hallway in the opposite direction.

Finally, he heard the faint *thump* of the boom box and knew he was getting close to the soldiers painting the World Trade Center mural. He rounded a corner and saw the soldier who'd given him the better-you-than-me look. It seemed to Matt like he'd been wandering the halls for hours, but there was the same guy, eating the same bag of Doritos.

The guy nudged one of his buddies and said something

to the group. The others dropped their tools and stood at attention, their hands held in a rigid salute, their gaze fixed on something outside the window. As Matt drew closer he saw what they were looking at: a black body bag being lifted into a transport.

Matt stopped, brought his hand to his brow, and watched. A sickening sensation came over him. The half-full body bag he'd seen earlier: It was Ali's.

MATT'S HEAD WAS ACHING AND HIS LEG WAS DRAGGING WORSE than ever as he trudged down the hall. When he walked into the ward, he saw Francis stuffing his belongings into a duffel bag. "What are you doing?" Matt asked.

"They're sending me back out," Francis said, jamming a pair of socks into the bag.

"I don't get it," Matt said.

Francis glanced around the room. "They say they've got some shit on me," he said. "Controlled substances, you know what I mean? They say I'm a wack job. That no one's going to believe me because of, you know . . ." He picked up an orange prescription bottle and gave it a shake. "I think I know who ratted on me: that prick with the yo-yo."

Matt looked over at Clarence. He was sound asleep.

And then Francis was gone, without a word of good-bye, Miss Piggy peeking out from the top of his duffel.

It was midday when Matt showed up outside Meaghan Finnerty's office. She was just packing up to go to lunch.

"Can we . . ." he started. "I really need to . . . can you talk for a couple minutes?"

"Five minutes," she said. "I've got five minutes. Then I have to be somewhere."

He closed the door, then sat across from her, watching the second hand on the clock inch forward. Before he knew it, he'd already wasted one of his five minutes.

"What we say in here, it's confidential, right?" he said finally.

She nodded.

He waited another thirty seconds. "I could be in big trouble," he said at last. Then he hurried on to the next sentence. "But I also think maybe I might not be in trouble at all."

She furrowed her brow.

"Ali," he said. "They know about it."

"They?"

"Lieutenant Colonel Fuchs and Lieutenant Brody." He waited a moment to see if her expression gave anything away. If she nodded, it would mean she'd been talking with Fuchs and Brody about him. If she looked surprised, it would mean she'd kept their conversations private like she'd said she would. But she didn't do either. She just waited for him to go on. Matt got up and started pacing.

"Some of the locals came to see them," he said. "They told them Ali was dead."

He stopped. He'd just said it out loud. It was real now. He felt his stomach seize up again.

"You okay?" Meaghan Finnerty said.

Matt nodded.

"Why don't you start at the beginning. Tell me what happened today."

He sat down and explained about being called into Fuchs's office. "Fuchs said they were going to question me, that there'd be an investigation," Matt said. "But then he told me to 'rethink' things. He said, 'You just can't be sure.' What does that mean?"

Meaghan Finnerty folded her arms across her chest. "I think it means exactly that."

He just looked at her.

"You *can't* be sure," she said. "You've said so yourself.

107

That things don't add up. That you can only remember bits and pieces. Fuchs is right. You can't be sure."

Matt didn't hesitate. "I need to be sure," he said.

Meaghan sighed. "Matt, terrible things happen out there," she said, gesturing to the invisible world beyond the Green Zone. "I can't tell you how many men come into this office and can't remember what happened to them. And then there are the ones who can't forget. Either way, it's torture."

"Please." He clasped his hands together, almost as if he were praying. "Help me."

She stood up and turned away from him. A few minutes passed. Then she turned around. "I'll try, Matt," she said. "But it's possible that your own mind might be your biggest enemy."

He cocked his head sideways.

"Your mind may be protecting you," she said. "Blocking out things it can't process."

Matt thought about this for a minute. "Then why do I keep seeing . . . things?"

"Why don't you tell me about these things?"

Matt looked at the clock. His five minutes were up five minutes ago. "Right now?"

"Right now."

He swallowed. "You won't tell anyone?"

She shook her head.

He looked away, scanned the walls of her tiny office, then fixed his gaze on a blank spot on the wall. "I was in this alley," he said slowly. "There was an abandoned car. And a candy wrapper snagged on a piece of razor wire. And shots," he said. "They ricocheted off the pavement. Then they got closer and I remember plaster falling down on my helmet. And this dog walking right through the whole thing."

He paused.

"All of a sudden, Ali's there. He's up at the other end of the alley where the shots are coming from. It's like one of those dreams where a person shows up somewhere they can't possibly be and yet in the dream it makes sense?"

She nodded.

"And then," he said, "there's a flash and it's like the light lifts him up. It's real slow and kind of beautiful in a way, the way he floats up into the light. And he looks happy at first. And then   then he starts waving his arms. . . ."

He couldn't finish. The sounds of the city drifted in—the rumble of traffic, kids shouting as they chased one another around the yard. Matt swallowed and went on.

"But I don't remember shooting my weapon." Matt covered his face with his hands. "I can remember other parts," he said. "What I can't remember is, you know . . ."

"Matt," she said gently.

He uncovered his eyes.

Meaghan leaned forward in her chair. "When something is too painful to process," she said gently, "your mind has a way of burying it."

Neither of them could say what "it" was. Shooting a child. Aiming, pulling the trigger, and killing a little boy.

AT CHURCH BACK HOME, MATT USED TO LOVE SLIPPING INSIDE the confessional booth—a cool, dark box where he knelt in silence waiting for the faint shushing sound that meant the priest had opened the screen between them.

"Please bless me, Father, for I have sinned," he would whisper.

He loved the honesty of those few words. As far as he was concerned, that *was* confession. Everything that followed—a recitation of sins, a penance of five Hail Marys or six Our Fathers—was predictable. But that first phrase—please bless me, Father, for I have sinned— was so humbling and so total, Matt always felt a kind of absolution as soon as he said it.

Confessions in Iraq were different, an impromptu talk with a battlefield chaplain or, more often, a late-night conversation with a buddy. But those conversations, where the inky black Iraqi night was lit by the embers of a pair of cigarettes, were somehow more sacred than anything he'd ever experienced in a church back home.

Secrets were confessed, not in the formal words prescribed by the Catholic Church but in combat slang: *I dropped a guy today. I lit up a house.* Or just *I did some sick shit today.*

Here at the hospital, there was no confessional: just a pair of metal folding chairs face-to-face in a hospital supply closet that had been commandeered for an hour. Matt sat down in the chair opposite Father Brennan and waited for a signal to begin. Meanwhile, the priest sat, his Oakland A's hat pulled low on his brow, his eyes intentionally fixed on the floor, as if to re-create the kind of anonymity of a real confessional.

"Please bless me, Father," Matt said, finally. "For I have sinned."

He didn't feel anything. No relief. Nothing. He didn't know what to say next. Back home, he would confess to swearing, to taking a soda from the vending machine at work, to being disrespectful to his mom. How did you confess to killing someone?

Matt wiped his hands on the front of his pants. He took a deep breath. He looked over his shoulder to make sure the closet door was closed, that no one was outside listening in.

He started all over again. "Please bless me, Father . . ." He couldn't finish.

He closed his eyes and tried to summon up every detail—to punish himself, to get it all out. He imagined the alley, blinding in the midday sun. But the rest—the dog, the sparks hitting the pavement, the overturned car—wouldn't come.

Meanwhile, his brain was besieged by random, maddening thoughts: Fuchs saying "You just can't be sure." Caroline asking if he wanted On the Go packets of Crystal Light. The year the World Series was postponed because of an earthquake. Was it 1998? Or 1989?

He opened his eyes. Father Brennan was still there, still bent forward, his eyes fixed on the floor.

Matt sighed. "I'm sorry, Father," he said. "I can't. I just can't . . ." His voice trailed off.

He stood up and paced around the tiny space. He took in the neatly folded piles of sheets and towels, the suture kits in their sterile bags, the bandages and bedpans. Then he looked at the pale, vulnerable skin at the base of Father Brennan's neck where his tan stopped, as he sat—resolutely, respectfully—staring at the floor.

Finally, the priest looked up. He took off his baseball hat and began twisting it between his hands. There was a sadness in his bright blue eyes but no judgment, no impatience.

"I'll be here," he said. "When you're ready."

MATT WALKED OUT OF THE SUPPLY ROOM AND TOOK A FEW steps. He stopped, considered turning around to try again, then continued on. He still had twenty minutes before his appointment with Lieutenant Brody, so he stepped outside into the courtyard and sat on the low wall where he and Pete sometimes met for a smoke.

He got out his notebook and turned to the page where he'd written a new version of what had happened, a version that included what he now knew.

1. *taxi runs the checkpoint*
2. *Justin and I pursue the vehicle*
3. *we turn down a side road, past the bootleg store*
4. *we get out of the Humvee to give chase down an alley*
5. *we get separated*

6. *I start taking fire in the alley*
7. *I return fire*
8. *Justin picks off the shooter from an upstairs window*
9. *RPG hits wall, Justin drags me to safety*

He didn't write about what happened when he returned fire. He couldn't.

He thought about what Meaghan had said about his brain protecting him from the truth. She'd also said something when he was leaving about how all soldiers struggle with their conscience when they do things in war that they'd never do otherwise.

All soldiers? Matt wondered. He and Wolf had had long conversations, often late into the night when neither of them could sleep, about what they'd seen and done in Iraq. But some of the other guys in the squad seemed untroubled by it all.

Figueroa, who had a wife and a kid he sang some Spanish lullaby to when he called home, had no qualms about it. "When you point your gun at someone and pull the trigger," he said, "shit happens. It's not a surprise. It's not pretty, but it's not something I necessarily want to talk about."

Justin just said he tried not to think about it too much. "When the bullets are whizzing by and it's all fucking chaos and noise, you don't think about morals or politics or anything. You *stop* thinking. And just fight. Because, just for those few seconds, it's simple: If you don't kill the other guy, he's going to kill you."

But Wolf was the one who surprised Matt the most. "I hate it, you know. I hate this shit. I hate how we came over here to help these people and instead we're killing them. But you know what else? I also sorta love it, man. When you're out there with your M16 and your night-vision goggles, you feel like you're ten feet tall and bulletproof. You are Superman. It's this primal thing. I love it. And I hate it."

Matt missed them, even Charlene, but he especially missed the guys. Their stupid "Don't Ask, Don't Tell" jokes. Their insults. He even missed the way the guys sat around burping and scratching their balls and just being gross. What he missed most, though, was the bravado, the cocky swagger they all adopted when they were shooting the breeze together. It might have been an act half the time, especially when they were heading into a dicey situation, but it was contagious.

And it was something he could use. Especially since he was due at Brody's office in five minutes.

MATT HAD HAD TO RUSH OUT OF THE HOSPITAL, ACROSS THE courtyard, and through the labyrinth of halls to get to Brody's office, his right leg dragging more and more the farther he went, and so he was sweating by the time he got there. He took a minute to catch his breath, then knocked.

Brody opened the door so quickly, it was almost as if he'd been standing on the other side just waiting for Matt's arrival. His office was much smaller than Fuchs's, more government-issue than former palace: a metal desk and chair, a filing cabinet and laptop. The only personal item in the room was a crucifix on a blank wall behind his desk.

"Private Duffy," he said, gesturing for Matt to sit in a chair in front of his desk. He grabbed a file and clicked his ballpoint pen into the ready position, as swiftly as if he were taking the safety off his gun. The friendly, proud-to-meet-you tone of their last meeting was gone.

"Before we begin . . ." he said, "let me tell you that the army takes this kind of accusation very seriously. And that we do our level best to get to the bottom of it."

Matt swallowed.

"Let me also explain that you will be held account-able for the facts not as they are in hindsight but as they appeared to you at the time."

Matt nodded as if he understood. The words sounded ominous, promising, and bureaucratic all at once. The facts in hindsight? Brody opened the file and began read-ing. "We understand that you and Private Justin Kane were in pursuit of a driver who had demonstrated hostile intent," he said, not looking up. "And that you were in advance of your squad without an officer present, due to the emergent nature of the threat and a shortage of officers in your sector at the time."

Matt rubbed his forehead with his hand. He tried to remember. Where was Sergeant McNally that day? Had he been at the checkpoint with them? And what did Brody mean, that there was a shortage of officers?

"We also understand," Brody went on, "that you and Private Kane pursued the insurgents through the area near the al-Hikma Mosque until they arrived at an alley. At which point you gave chase on foot. The enemy opened fire, and you and Private Kane set up a position in a building across the street from the sniper."

Matt tried to keep up with Brody's rapid-fire recita-tion while at the same time trying to square what Brody was saying with what he remembered. He still had no recollection of the building they went into.

"Private Kane neutralized the target, at which point the two of you exited the building to return to your vehicle and make radio contact with your squad," he said. "Then an RPG was fired in the proximity of your position, immobilizing you in the alley." He looked at Matt briefly, as if to make sure that Matt understood that he was the "you" he was talking about. "Renewed fighting erupted and Private Kane, with no regard for his own safety, ran through intermittent fire to rescue you . . ."

Intermittent fire. Justin hadn't mentioned any shooting after the RPG went off. Justin had made it sound like the fighting was over once he took out the sniper, that the RPG was a single, parting shot as the insurgents took off. Justin had run through gunfire to save him. Matt was stunned.

". . . during the course of the engagement that day." Brody had come to the end of a sentence that sounded important, Matt realized, and he tried to focus. "There were, unfortunately, civilian casualties: an elderly man and the youth, Ayyad Mahmud Aladdin Kimadi."

Brody paused for a split-second, flipped to a page in the back of the file, then peered at Matt.

"I understand that you've been experiencing some memory problems." It was a statement but also a question.

"Yes, sir," Matt said.

"Some difficulties with recognizing dates and times? Some anterograde amnesia?"

"Yes, sir," he said. "I think so. Sir." He thought it was anterograde, not the other one, but he didn't dare check his notebook, not after what Meaghan had said.

"And so your recollection of the chain of events would not be considered reliable." Brody's tone made it clear that this was not a question.

Matt held his breath. He had memorized each thing that had occurred that day in the alley as best as he could determine it, using the numbered list in his notebook the same way he'd memorized the World Series trivia. He'd crammed all morning and he was ready, he hoped, to answer Brody's questions.

Brody sighed. "It's unfortunate," he said. "But this is what happens when insurgents put their own people in harm's way."

Matt nodded. Mentally, he reviewed the wording of the Rules of Engagement. *Do not fire into civilian-populated areas or buildings unless the enemy is using them for military purposes or if necessary for your self-defense.*

He also repeated to himself what Sergeant Benson had told them as they were about to enter Iraq. He'd made them all pause at the border and turn off their engines for a little pep talk. "You are going to get shot at," he'd said. "It's going to come down to him or you. Better him than you."

Brody closed the file and stood up. "Let me tell you about an incident that happened the other day near the Jamila Market," he said.

What was going on? Was Brody trying to confuse him?

"A driver comes to our southern checkpoint, asks permission to park in one of the busiest areas in the market," he said. "He has three kids in the backseat. Little ones. Says he has to carry something from one of the stalls to his car and he doesn't want to leave the kids alone in the parking lot."

Matt squinted, trying to follow what Brody was saying.

"Our guys waved him in, helped him park. He walks away. Couple minutes later, the car blows up. With the kids still in the back."

Matt winced. He should have realized where the story was heading, but it didn't matter. He was shocked every time he heard a story like that.

"These people," Brody said. "They just don't value life here the way we do." He shook his head and went on. "Private Duffy, you know what collateral damage is, don't you?"

Matt nodded. It was an army term for all the

nonmilitary things that get destroyed by war—roads, factory buildings, sewage plants. Even livestock. It was also a euphemism the army used when one of its bombs ended up killing civilians.

"Well, that's what we have here. A classic case of collateral damage."

Matt mentally went over what he would say. He would explain about how he was pinned down. How, somehow, he was alone in the alley.

Brody cleared his throat. "We could spend a year trying to figure out what happened here. And it wouldn't matter. Because it's the insurgents who endanger civilians. By operating in their midst."

Matt just looked at him.

"We can't go back to the Hikma sector to collect ballistics; it's become too unstable in the past few days," he said. "The witnesses, if there were any, have probably already been coached—or bribed or threatened. And the body won't tell us anything: You look the same if you get killed by an enemy bullet or an American bullet."

Matt cringed. He pictured the body bag he'd seen the other day and wondered, for the one hundredth time, what Ali's body might have looked like.

Sometime during this speech, Brody had gone to sit down behind his desk. He tapped the on button on his computer and it whirred to life.

He stared at the screen for a moment or two, then looked up at Matt. "That will be all, Private," he said. "Time to get back to the business we came here for."

And, Matt realized sluggishly, that he was supposed to stand, salute, and leave.

But it wasn't until he had left, until he'd traveled down the hall a few steps, that it sunk in that Brody had *told* him what had happened. Brody hadn't asked him a single question.

MATT WANDERED A LITTLE FARTHER DOWN THE HALL, THEN stopped at a spot where several hallways met. He took in the labyrinth of halls, utterly lost.

A few yards down the hallway to his left, he saw a men's room. He walked slowly toward it, stepped inside, and considered what to do next. He closed the seat on one of the toilets, sat down, and leaned his head back against the cool marble wall.

His eyes closed, he tried to understand what had just happened. What had Brody said about Matt's memory? That his recollection of the chain of events "would not be considered reliable"? Is that why he hadn't asked Matt any questions? So where did he get all the other information? From Justin?

Brody had called Ali an enemy sympathizer. But that's what they always said when a civilian got killed.

He'd also said there was a shortage of officers that day. Classic cover-your-ass language intended to keep any blame off the higher-ups.

But Brody hadn't actually blamed anyone. What had he said? Something like, "That's what happens when insurgents put civilians in harm's way."

And the last thing he'd said was something about getting back to business. Did that mean Matt was cleared? That he was being sent back to his squad?

Matt got up, walked to the sink, and splashed cold water on his face. He knew he should be relieved. But his head ached and he had a hollow, uneasy feeling in his gut.

He regarded himself in the mirror. His complexion was gray, his eyes hooded. The cold, impassive face that stared out at him looked like a mug shot.

Matt turned around, took a step, then flung open a stall door and retched.

WHEN MATT GOT BACK TO THE WARD, THERE WAS A NEW GUY in Francis's bed. He was a small, wiry guy with ginger-colored hair and a pale complexion.

"Hey," he called out as Matt walked past. "Want to see something cool?"

Matt stopped, more out of politeness than interest, and the guy picked up a plastic Dixie cup and shook it. Something rattled around inside, something hard. As Matt leaned in, he saw that it was a piece of shrapnel, roughly the size and shape of a lima bean.

"This was inside me," the guy said, lifting his shirt to show a bandage on his belly. "Cool, huh?"

"Yeah," Matt said, barely looking. He couldn't stand this guy. Not because he was being such a little girl about his injury. Because he was in Francis's bed. "Real cool."

THAT NIGHT, AFTER HIS MIND HAD FINALLY WOUND DOWN and he'd drifted into a fitful sleep, Matt woke abruptly. He sat up, trying to figure out what had roused him from his sleep. The ward was absolutely silent. And, that, he realized, was what had awoken him. There was no crying. He listened for a long time, until he understood. The person crying each night must have been Francis.

MATT WAS WAITING OUTSIDE MEAGHAN FINNERTY'S OFFICE when she came in the next morning.

"You told him I couldn't remember, didn't you?" he said. "Brody. You told him."

A vague look of irritation crossed her face, but she didn't answer. She simply opened her bag and fished around for her keys. She pulled them out, opened the office, and waved Matt in.

"You talked to him, didn't you?" Matt said as soon as they were inside her office.

125

Meaghan closed the door, then walked around her desk and sat down. But she still didn't say anything.

"I thought you said that what we talked about in here was private."

"I also told you my job was to evaluate you," she said. Her tone was crisp.

"So did you?" he asked.

"Did I what?"

"Did you evaluate me?"

She nodded. "I told him you were ready to go back to your unit."

The words hit Matt like a flying brick. But he worked hard to keep his gaze steady, not to blink, not to swallow, not to give a single hint of the panic that was stealing over him. What if he wasn't really ready?

The one thing that had kept him going these past few days was the idea of getting back to his buddies. Now he was terrified. Afraid of leaving the calm, orderly world of the hospital. Afraid that he'd be overwhelmed by the chaos of the streets. Afraid of being afraid.

That was what worried him most. That he wouldn't be able to fire his gun.

He quickly pushed the idea to a corner of his mind. He was going back to the squad. To Justin, Wolf, Figueroa, and Charlene. That was all that really mattered.

Meaghan Finnerty folded her arms across her chest.

There was an air of finality about her gesture, a signal, it seemed, that their business was finished. Still, it looked like there was something she wasn't saying.

Finally, she pushed her chair back and stood up. Matt stood slowly, his right leg trembling ever so slightly. Meaghan Finnerty stared into his eyes and for a moment he saw a flicker of the warmth she'd shown him in the past. Then she snapped her hand to her brow in a crisp salute. It was a startling gesture, completely at odds with army protocol for an officer, even a junior officer, to salute a private.

Matt raised his hand to his forehead and returned the salute. "Thank you," he said quietly. "Ma'am."

It wasn't until he'd pulled the door closed behind him and walked away that he understood. Meaghan Finnerty had protected him. She'd told Brody that his memory was unreliable—precisely so he *wouldn't* be questioned.

And she was sending him back to his squad. She'd decided that he was ready. She'd never told him what she thought about Ali's death. But she must have determined that he was, as she'd once put it, not a danger to himself, his fellow soldiers, or the Iraqi people.

"WELL, PRIVATE, DID YOU ENJOY YOUR STAY HERE?" KWONG said, scribbling something in Matt's chart.

Matt tried to remember how many times he'd seen Kwong since he'd arrived at the hospital.

"Looks like everything is in order," Kwong said. "Except for the minibar tab. You'll have to settle that on your way out."

Matt gave him a weak, obligatory smile.

"I'm going to send you back with some meds," Kwong said, scratching something on a prescription pad.

"What for?" Matt said.

"Headaches. They might come back, especially if you're exposed to loud noise or bright sunlight."

Matt wondered for a minute if this was a joke. Machine gunfire, explosions, and the roar of heavy vehicles. That was all you heard in the field—as you stood out under a harsh, unforgiving sun. But Kwong wasn't joking. He was looking squarely at Matt with concern etched on his face.

"And keep an eye on that right leg," he said. "It's nothing major, but it could slow you down out there."

Matt's mouth fell open slightly.

"You thought I didn't notice, didn't you?" Kwong was smiling, but he didn't look happy exactly. He hung the clipboard on the foot of the bed, then handed Matt the prescription. "Take care of yourself out there, Private. I don't want to see you back here."

"HERE," NURSE McCRAE SAID LATER WHEN SHE CAME BY TO write up Matt's discharge report. She was holding out a satellite phone. "You get to call home again. To tell them you're going back."

Matt looked at the clock; it was almost midnight at home. He punched in all the international dialing codes, then waited.

His sister picked up. "Matty?" she said. "Is that you? Hey. I got my learner's permit."

"Wow." Matt's voice was flat, distracted. "Great."

"You don't sound that excited," she said. In the background, Gym Class Heroes were singing about taking their clothes off.

"Turn that down, will you?" he said. "Yeah, I'm excited, I guess. I just feel sorry for all those other drivers out there."

"Very funny," Lizzy said. "So can I use your car? You

said, once I got my learner's—"

He stopped her before she could repeat the entire speech. "Yeah," he said. "But only if you take Mom out with you."

"Social suicide." When Lizzy was annoyed with him, she didn't use verbs or full sentences, for that matter.

"All right," he said. "Take Brandon. But tell him I'll kill him if, you know, if anything happens—"

"Thankyouthankyouthank—"

"—to you."

There was a pause. "Jeez, Matt," Lizzy said. "When did you turn into, like, a Hallmark card?"

"I don't know." He tried to think of something sarcastic to say back to her, but nothing, it seemed, was funny.

"You okay?" Lizzy said. "Mom says you have, like, a concussion."

"Yeah, something like that. But I'm fine," he said. "Tell Mom . . . tell Mom I'm going back to my unit."

"Oh." It was quiet on the other end. "Be careful, Matty."

There was a crackle in the line, followed by a swift series of computerized beeps. Call waiting. Probably Brandon.

"And Lizzy, tell Mom to make sure everyone uses the side door from now on," he said.

"What?"

"Use the side door. Tell everyone to use the side door."

"Why?"

"You want my car or not? Just do what I said, okay?"

The line bristled with static again. Time to go. Time to let his little sister get back to her life. Matt coughed.

"Love you, Lizard," he said.

"I love you, too, Matty."

The line beeped, then went silent, as if the digital tether that had linked his hospital room in Saddam's old palace to Lizzy's bedroom back home had suddenly snapped.

HE BROUGHT THE PHONE TO NURSE MCCRAE AND ASKED FOR paper and an envelope. Then he went back to his bed and wrote to Caroline.

Dear Caroline,

Thanks for the baby wipes. It seems like sissy stuff to use them, but they help. They really do.

I think my ma already told you, but I got hurt a while ago. Nothing bad, though. I just banged up

*my head a little. And now I'm leaving the hospital
to go back to the guys.*

*This is a strange place. You think there are
rules and there's right and wrong and you think
officers are all assholes who only want to make
your life miserable. And then you find out that
everybody has a different idea of what's right
and wrong. And that a lot of people act like they
want to know what's going on but that they really
don't—because then they might have to do something about it. Like I said, it's strange.*

*I miss the guys and I wonder what it will be
like when I get back out there. I just hope that
being in here didn't make me go soft or anything.
Apparently the army thinks my brain is okay
enough for me to go back out and shoot a gun
again. I hope they're right.*

He crossed out the last line. Then he reread the letter—
and crumpled it into a ball and threw it in the trash.
Caroline wouldn't have any idea what he was talking
about. He wasn't sure *he* really knew what he was talking about.

He wanted to tell her about Francis—about how what
happened with his squad leader had made him crazy.
And he wanted to tell her about Meaghan Finnerty—
about how she was still sort of a mystery to him. He

wanted to tell her how the army makes everybody walk this line between talking about things and not talking about them. And how confusing it all was. His thoughts ran laps around themselves. Until finally they landed on something simple.

He started a new letter to Caroline.

> *Dear Caroline,*
> *How was the bio quiz?*

THE WIPE BOARD AT THE NURSES' STATION SAID FATHER Brennan was holding confessions in the linen closet again, so Matt decided to stop by and get a blessing before he left.

The door was ajar and he saw the priest kneeling on the floor, his baseball cap in his hands. Matt didn't say a word; he simply got down on his knees next to the priest.

It was like being an altar boy again. There was something very simple and real about kneeling to pray—nothing like the hasty "Dear Gods" he muttered in the middle of a firefight. And so Matt closed his eyes and waited. Waited to feel better, to feel the calm, the comfort that used to descend on him when he was an altar boy. He'd never told anyone, but he believed, really believed, that what he felt in that moment was grace.

No words of prayer came to him. But that was fine. And he didn't feel the grace he'd hoped for, but after a while, after a few minutes of kneeling there, his eyes closed, the frantic hospital sound track faded to a hush, and something shifted in him. He couldn't say what it was, but he felt lighter somehow when he finally opened his eyes and stood.

The priest stood, too, stiffly. He lifted his hand above Matt and made the sign of the cross over him, then touched his purple stole to Matt's forehead.

Matt reached inside his pants pocket and pulled out the small box that held his medal. He handed it, without a word, to the priest. He hadn't planned on this, but it felt right.

Father Brennan accepted it, simply, and without question. "I'll hold on to this for you, son," he said. "Until you're ready."

THE CHATTER OF CRICKETS. THAT WAS ONE OF THE THINGS Matt had forgotten about life back in Sadr City. How sometimes, in the middle of the night, when all the shelling and shooting had stopped, crickets would pipe up, relaying information back and forth to each other in an eerie, high-pitched frequency all their own.

He'd also forgotten the dust. How it got into everything, how it settled in between each strand of hair on your head, how it got between your teeth. And the smell. The constant smell of burning garbage, the sickly stench of raw sewage. And, of course, the heat, how it seared your throat when you took a deep breath.

But then there was the comfortable weight of Itchy's warm, purring body at the foot of his cot. And the sound of Figueroa's snoring, the rhythmic in-and-out that allowed Matt to pretend all was well with the world. And the birdsong at daylight, a sign that somehow they'd all made it through another night.

Their base camp looked pretty much the same. At some point during the time Matt was gone, the guys had spray-painted a bedsheet with the words *Camp Benson* and hung it over the door, naming the barracks after their first squad leader. And Wolf's mom had sent a dartboard with plastic suction-cup darts, which the guys had been shooting at a poster of Saddam. But other than that, things were strangely the same.

The guys had been really happy to see him. Wolf was the first one to spot him as his Humvee pulled up.

"Dude," he called out. "You look like you just went three rounds on *Jerry Springer.*"

Matt climbed out of the Humvee and went to give Wolf a hug.

"Whoa there, dog," Wolf said. "You know I have intimacy issues." Then he grabbed Matt around the neck and gave him a big, noisy fake kiss. "I hope that doesn't make you feel dirty," he said, grabbing Matt's duffel bag and hoisting it over his shoulder. "C'mon in," he said. "We've got an ice-cold Bud waiting for you."

When Matt walked in, the guys were sitting around watching *Rambo: First Blood Part II* on Justin's DVD player. They were just at the part where the exploding arrows blow up the Vietnamese soldiers; it was one of the best scenes, but everybody jumped up to welcome him back.

Figueroa came running at him like a linebacker and picked him up off his feet. All the other guys gathered around and smacked him on the back, the chest—any part they could get a hold of. Justin smacked his butt and Matt took a fake swipe at him as Figueroa set him back down on the ground.

"Oooh, I like that," Justin said. "You're sexy when you're angry."

Even Charlene fussed over him, giving him one of those hugs where you technically hug the other person while barely touching them. When they pulled away from each other, she studied the bruises on his face. "I have one word for you, dude," she said. "Concealer."

"What happened while I was gone?" Matt had said later as they all sat around, eating Wisconsin Chocolate Cow Pies, salami, and Fruity Pebbles straight from the box—all part of a going-away care package Pete had given him. He'd also thrown in some Stay Alert Gum, some Febreze, and an Operation Iraqi Freedom Christmas Ornament, packed with Kotex pads to protect it.

"Did you guys win the war or something? It's so quiet."

"Didn't you hear?" Charlene said. "There's a cease-fire in our sector. Thirty days. We have eighteen to go."

"You shitting me?" Matt said.

"That is the authentic truth," Justin said.

"Dog, that was the word of the day last week," said Wolf. "What's today's word?"

Justin sort of grimaced. *"Kundalini."*

The place erupted. Figueroa laughed so hard, he spit out his soda.

Wolf put his arm around Justin. "Nah, dude, that's your mother's favorite sexual position."

"No, Wolfman," Justin came right back at him. "That's what your girlfriend and I were doing last night!"

They'd goofed around most of the day—playing

cards, catching up on their sleep, and writing home—
since Bravo Company was handling street patrols while
their group got a little break during the cease-fire. No
one had really talked too much about Matt getting
hurt, and he wondered if they even knew what happened in the alley. Or did they know about what Matt
had done and just decided not to talk about it?

Now they were all asleep, all except for the new
guy, Mitchell, a thick-necked kid from Georgia, who
was standing guard outside the barracks door. And
Matt lay in bed with Itchy curled up at his feet wondering if this cease-fire would hold, if maybe it meant
the war was going to be over soon, if he wouldn't have
to worry about whether or not he'd be able to fire his
gun when the time came.

"HEY, DUDE, YOU WANT TO PLAY HALO?" MATT SAID THE
next morning when he saw Justin heating up a ham-and-
egg MRE omelet on the engine of the truck.

The two of them had spent hours, probably days,
playing Halo, with Matt driving the Mongoose and Justin
manning the gun. Sometimes, they teamed up against
Wolf and Figueroa, but mainly it was just the two of

them. Playing Halo was one of the things Matt had missed most when he was in the hospital. That, and just hanging out with Justin. But since Matt had gotten back, things seemed different somehow. Matt wasn't sure, maybe he was being paranoid, but he felt like Justin was avoiding being alone with him.

Justin picked up the foil-wrapped packet and flipped it over. "Nah, dude," he said. "I'm not that into Halo anymore."

"Oh." Matt took a step back. He looked off toward the horizon, trying to think of something to say, some way to ease back into the way things used to be between them, some way to talk about what happened.

Justin grabbed the MRE off the engine. "Later," was all he said as he walked away.

"I HAVE AN IDEA," WOLF SAID THE NEXT NIGHT AFTER THEY'D finished watching the whole Rambo trilogy. They'd already let the air out of Figueroa's air mattress while he was taking a nap and eaten everything in the care package, even the Healthy Ways fiber mix. They were bored. And restless. Like kindergarten kids inside on a rainy day. "Let's play capture the flag," he said.

Figueroa glanced up from reading *Let God Handle It*, the book he called his bible, and groaned. Justin pretended to yawn, opening his mouth and patting it with his hand.

"No, you guys don't get it," Wolf said as he stood up, put on his helmet, and donned his night-vision goggles. "In our NVGs."

At that, they all jumped up. All except Charlene.

"You'll be in trouble when McNally gets back," she said.

"Jeez, Charlene," Wolf said. "You sound like the fish in that Dr. Seuss book where the things come and mess up the house." He put his hands on his hips. "'I do not like this. Not one little bit.'"

Even Charlene couldn't help but smile and watch as they put on their NVGs and ran outside to what used to be a large playground when the school was actually a school. They invited some of the guys from Charlie Company to join them so they'd have enough players, divided into two teams, and decided that one "flag" would be Mitchell's Georgia Tech pennant and the other would be a thong some girl had given Wolf. Then they separated into the pitch-black Iraqi night.

The last time Matt had worn his NVGs was months ago. He tried to remember which month, but he couldn't come up with even a clue to help him recall it and quickly dropped the idea. It left him with an uneasy feeling, though, a low-grade anxiety about his memory, something he pushed to a corner of his mind as he joined the game.

The world, as seen through night-vision goggles, was a spooky, video-game landscape in shades of black and green, where people's eyes glowed like white pinpricks of light and where moving figures looked like ghosts trailing wisps of bright, fluorescent green. Any sudden light, like the flash of a muzzle or the blowback of an explosion, was blinding—at least for a few seconds.

It took Matt a little while to get reaccustomed to the murky green view and, as he walked into the playground, he felt slightly dizzy. After a few minutes, though, he was in the flow, playing attacker as he snuck across the border—a line they'd drawn in the dirt dividing the playground in two—and running toward the thong, which he'd seen Wolf hide under an old ammunition crate. He was aware, as he made a dash toward the crate, that his right leg was still not quite keeping up with his left, another thought he quickly disregarded.

He was just a few feet from the crate when a blinding white light flashed in his eyes. He fell back, stumbled, and landed on his butt. He could hear laughter coming from above and behind him, but he had no idea what had just happened.

"Private Duffy." The voice, low and gravelly, belonged to Sergeant McNally.

"Yes, sir." Matt struggled to his feet and pulled off his mask.

"I see you've recovered." McNally had been away at a battalion meeting the day before, so this was their first encounter since Matt's return. There was a hint of sarcasm in his tone as he extinguished his flashlight, which, Matt realized, had been what had blinded him a second ago.

"Yes, sir," Matt said as heartily as he could.

"And I suppose you think playing games with U.S. government equipment is a good idea." Matt could see Charlene, just over Sergeant McNally's shoulder, smirking.

"No, sir," Matt said.

"Private Anderson here"—he gestured toward Wolf—"said this was your idea."

Matt caught sight of Wolf grinning like a maniac behind McNally.

"Well, Private Duffy, I'd like to commend you for your creativity," McNally said. "This is a terrific little training drill for maintaining battle readiness during the cease-fire."

It took Matt a minute to register that McNally was actually okay with them goofing around in their NVGs, that he was basically giving them permission. Behind him, Charlene was rolling her eyes. Wolf was giving Matt the finger.

"All right then, men," McNally said. "Get back to the exercise." He walked away, then stopped and turned around. "Welcome back, Private Duffy."

Matt thanked him, then walked to the side of the playground and sat down on the ground. A little while later, Charlene came over and sat next to him. "You okay?"

He was winded, actually, and still a little unsteady after falling down. "Yeah, fine, no problem."

The two of them sat there in silence, watching as the guys kept playing. "I took care of your mangy little pet while you were gone," Charlene said finally.

Matt turned and looked at her. Maybe she wasn't so bad after all. Maybe she was actually trying to say she'd missed him. He leaned over and gave her a gentle shove with his shoulder.

"It's not like I like that cat or anything, Duffy," she said, watching as Figueroa ran by waving Mitchell's Georgia Tech pennant. "But pets can actually help reduce stress."

Matt did a double take. "What's that from, Charlene, some new field manual?"

"Yeah," she said, nudging him back. "Top secret."

Justin was outside the barracks, shaving. He'd filled his helmet with water and was peering in the rearview mirror of a Humvee at his reflection.

"I am looking mighty fine today," he said as Matt walked up. "Mighty fine."

Matt scratched his head. "What was that word? You know, too much pride?"

Justin didn't miss a beat. "*Hubris*, my man," he said, drawing the razor across his jawline. "Overbearing pride. Presumption."

"Yeah," Matt said. "That. What you just said."

Justin dipped the razor into the water. "No, dog. It isn't hubris when you're as good-looking as me." He flicked the razor in Matt's direction, splashing his face with a few tepid drops of water.

Matt stood there, watching him. He squinted at the heat waves rising off the pavement. "Good day to go to the beach," he said.

Justin didn't answer. He was concentrating on his upper lip.

"So, dude . . ." Matt couldn't just start talking about it. He tried to think of a way to ease into the conversation.

The worst thing he could do was act like he really needed to talk. "You, uh . . . you were right about the Green Zone."

Justin raised an eyebrow at his reflection in the rearview mirror. "Oh, yeah?"

"Yeah, dude. Did you see all that marble? How 'bout that chandelier in the . . ." He couldn't remember the word. The room where all the cots and Porta Potties were, the giant room with the turquoise dome and the balcony.

Justin had nearly finished shaving. He smoothed his palm over his cheek, checking for spots he might have missed.

"Ballroom!" Matt said. "The ballroom."

Justin dumped the rinse water out onto the ground, where it evaporated pretty much the minute it hit the dirt. Then he pulled his nerdy black glasses out of his shirt pocket, put them on, and regarded himself in the mirror again. "Damn, I'm even more handsome when I can really see myself."

He flicked a few drops of liquid off the razor, then turned and went inside.

THE SQUAD WAS BACK ON PATROL THE NEXT DAY, WALKING the beat in the market. It was the first time Matt had put all his gear on since he got back and he was sweating before they even left the base.

"Duffy," McNally had said, "you pair up with Charlene today. I want you to take it easy."

Charlene had huffed a little behind McNally's back, insulted, as usual, at the implication that her role was somehow easier than everyone else's. And to prove it, she set an unnecessarily fast pace as they walked the aisles of the market.

The market was different somehow. There were more people, more stalls, more goods for sale. Crates of shiny yellow lemons, sneakers, bolts of fabric, trays of tea. It was the cease-fire, Matt realized. The people also seemed different: The fearful, suspicious looks they often showed the soldiers seemed to be largely gone. Replaced with relief, even indifference. That, to Matt, seemed like the biggest sign of progress—that people were going about their daily lives without looking or even caring about the presence of American soldiers.

He was lagging well behind Charlene, though, and

rather than focus on the sights and smells of the market, Matt found he had to work to keep her in view, not an easy task given that she was shorter than most of the people in the market.

He spotted her a few stalls away and tried to pick up his pace. He tripped, though, and nearly went down on his knee. Quickly, he looked around to see if anyone had noticed, then jogged a little to catch up to Charlene.

A scrum of kids ran by, and Matt drew back instinctively. He saw Ali everywhere, in every kid on the street. He heard his voice every time one of the kids yelled, and he found himself flinching every time he heard the soft *pock* of someone kicking a soccer ball.

He stopped to catch his breath and decided to watch the kids for a minute; he couldn't avoid looking at them forever.

They were chasing a stray dog through the rows of stalls, throwing pebbles at it. Matt blinked. It was the dog from the alley, the one who'd been nosing through the trash right before . . . He blinked again, trying to shut the image out of his mind.

The dog yelped—one of the stones had hit him— then doubled back in Matt's direction. The animal came so close that his tail brushed against Matt's leg. Matt jumped as if he'd been singed by fire. Then he saw that it wasn't the same dog at all. That this one had a curly tail, a neat curlicue of fur tipped in white.

Matt sagged against a wall and reached for the plastic straw on his CamelBak, the backpack hydration system all the guys had. He was roasting. And his head had started to ache.

"What's the matter with you, Duffy? Am I too much man for you?" It was Charlene. He'd never been so glad to see her.

Matt took another sip of water, then wiped his hand across his mouth, stalling for time. "Can we just stay here a minute?" he said finally. It was humiliating to have to ask Charlene, of all people, if they could take a break.

She rolled her eyes, then took a minute to look him over. For just a moment, though, he thought he saw a little hint of warmth in her eyes. Then she put her hands on her hips and sighed. "Roger that."

IT WAS UNUSUALLY COOL THAT NIGHT—ANOTHER THING THAT had surprised Matt when he first arrived in Iraq. How it could be sweltering all day, then cold at night. It was something he'd learned in basic training, but not something he'd understood until Justin explained it to him. There was no humidity in the desert, he'd said, so there was nothing to hold the heat; that meant that as soon as the sun set, it turned cold.

Especially on clear nights. Like tonight. But Wolf's mom had just sent him a care package with a fresh supply of Skoal and so Matt, Wolf, and Justin were sitting on a ledge outside having a dip. Matt was never a big Skoal man, but he'd decided to join them, mostly just to hang out with Justin.

"I love my ma," Wolf said, spitting a stream of tobacco juice into the dirt. "You gotta love a woman who knows her chaw."

"Yeah, dog. My ma sends me Grizzly," Justin said. "She said it's because they give you free shit, like key chains and beer mugs, but I know it's because it's cheap."

Matt had only put a small pinch in his mouth, but he was already feeling light-headed the way he had the first time he'd tried it. Must have been because he hadn't chewed in so long.

"I can't believe your mothers even send you this stuff," Matt said. "Moms are supposed to say that chewing tobacco is like the gateway drug for heroin."

Wolf laughed, then coughed and spit. "Yeah, she says it'll kill me, but she sends it to me, anyway."

The three of them sat there a little while, not saying anything.

"What do you think is worse?" Wolf said at last.

149

"Dying of cancer or getting hit by a car?"

"You're a sick shit, Wolf," Justin said. "Morbid. Obsessed with death."

"No, seriously," Wolf said. "Tell me you haven't thought about it. We're out here getting shot at and you don't think to yourself, you know, 'What if?'"

"I think about it sometimes," Matt said after a while. "I thought about it a lot after Benson."

Another long silence.

"Benson died fighting for our country," Justin finally said. "He died for us. I don't care how it went down, he died a beautiful death."

They were all quiet again. The only noises were the crickets and the occasional *pfffft* sound of one of them spitting into the dirt.

"If I'm going to die," Wolf said, "I want to be doing something important, something where they can say 'he died doing something for somebody else,' not in a plane crash or in, like, some drunk-driving accident."

The other two nodded. "You know what Johnny Rambo says, boys," Justin said. "'Live for nothing or die for something.'"

Matt had never really understood that line. He'd watched the whole Rambo trilogy a bunch of times, but he never quite got the "live for nothing" part. The whole squad quoted Rambo all the time and that was another thing that seemed weird to Matt: how when things in Iraq got confusing or deep, that the person they turned to was a fake action hero from the '80s.

MATT HAD TAKEN JUST ONE OF THE HEADACHE PILLS KWONG had given him, but his head was still pounding when he lay down to go to sleep. He was exhausted, though, and half sick from the chewing tobacco, and eventually he fell asleep.

Sometime during the night he heard a gunshot. A single *pop* from somewhere in the distance. He sat up and looked around to see if the other guys had heard it. But everyone else was asleep. Figueroa was snoring, as usual, and of course Itchy hadn't even stirred.

Matt wondered for a moment if he'd imagined it. And so he got up and walked outside to where Mitchell was standing guard.

"You hear anything?" he asked.

Mitchell shrugged his beefy shoulders. "Maybe," he said. "Yeah. Like one shot." He looked Matt up and down. "Nothing to interrupt your beauty sleep over."

Matt went back inside and tried to go back to sleep. But his headache was worse now than before. He fished

around in his duffel, gulped down a couple more headache pills, and tried to go back to sleep. Soon, though, he
heard the birds starting to twitter, and the pinkish light
of dawn crept into the barracks.

He got up, made some instant coffee, opened up a
stick of the Stay Alert Gum that Pete had given him,
and put it in his mouth. *One piece delivers one hundred
milligrams of caffeine five times faster than pills or coffee,*
the label said. *Stay Alert received the Army's Greatest
Invention of the Year Award for 2005.* Matt unwrapped
another stick and popped it in his mouth.

MATT INCHED THE DOOR OPEN SLOWLY, NOT WANTING TO
wake the other guys, and stepped outside. It wasn't even
seven, but it was already broiling and the sun was so
bright, it made him shrink back a little. When his eyes
adjusted he saw Charlene, in a wife-beater and gym
shorts, over by the truck lifting weights.

"Need a spotter?" he said as he walked over.

Charlene didn't answer. She set the dumbbells down
with a sigh. "You know I can bench-press more than half
the guys in this platoon?"

"Yes, Charlene, I think you told me that about a

hundred times." He nearly told her that he also heard she slept with a stuffed animal, but he decided not to piss her off.

He handed her his water bottle.

She squeezed some water into her mouth, then handed it back. "You're different now," she said, scowling slightly.

"Well, at least you're still Miss Congeniality," he said.

She looked away, and Matt wondered if maybe he'd hurt her feelings.

"Kidding," he said. "Just kidding. You're, I don't know, you're different, too."

She shot him a dubious look.

"You're . . . oh, jeez, Charlene, don't make me say it. Okay. You're nicer."

She winced. "I don't exactly aspire to be nice, Duffy."

Girls. Like Francis said, they were another species.

"Don't take this the wrong way, okay?" she said.

He shrugged.

"You're . . . I don't know." She looked off into the distance and Matt followed her gaze. Across the road from the school was an open field. It was littered with garbage. A few goats were grazing on whatever they could find. An old man was bent over at the waist,

153

rifling through the trash.

Charlene picked up the dumbbells and went back to her routine.

"I just want to be sure you're okay."

He could tell she was trying to sound casual. But there was nothing casual about Charlene.

"TODAY WE'RE GOING TO BE PATROLLING A DIFFERENT SECTOR," McNally had announced at their morning meeting. "The area around the al-Hikma Mosque."

That was the sector near the alley. As soon as McNally gave the orders, Matt had felt his throat tighten up. He stole a glance at Justin. If he had any reaction to the news, he wasn't showing it.

Now the whole squad was riding in the back of a Stryker, an armored vehicle, en route to their assignment, playing their favorite game. It didn't have a name and no one remembered quite how it started. But it was simple. One person came up with two names. Celebrities, usually, someone everyone knew. Then someone else predicted which one would win in a fight. There was no winner or loser in the game; it was just a way to kill time.

"David Spade versus Richard Simmons." This was

Figueroa's contribution. He was slightly older than the rest of the guys, so his choices were sometimes a little lame.

"Richard Simmons, for sure," said Wolf. "The dude works out." He struck a *Saturday Night Fever* pose. "Sweating to the Oldies."

The vehicle hit a bump, flew up in the air, and landed. They all froze for a second. Then, when nothing happened, when they weren't blown to smithereens by an IED, they seemed to exhale collectively.

Figueroa was the first one to speak. "What's that thing you're sitting on, Mitchell?"

Mitchell's cheeks turned red. "Hemorrhoid cushion," he said. "My grandma saw it advertised on some website that had, like, care packages for soldiers."

The others hooted with laughter.

"No shit," Mitchell said. "The website said it was good for protecting your ass on these bumpy roads."

"Let me try that," Wolf said.

Mitchell handed it to him. He had to. He was new.

Wolf sat on it and wiggled his butt around. The Stryker hit another bump, this time a small one. Wolf nodded his approval. "Tell your grandma to send me one, too."

They rode on a little farther. It was like an oven inside the back of the vehicle. Worse, they couldn't see what was going on outside. The Stryker slowed, then stopped.

This was the worst part. Whenever it stopped, they were sitting ducks.

Wolf got the game going again. "Kelly Ripa versus Mel B."

"Mel B?" Justin said. "Who the fuck is that?" Justin hadn't really been playing. He'd been tying and retying his laces, checking his gear, generally fidgeting.

"Scary Spice, dude."

"Jesus, Wolf!" Justin kicked the bench Wolf was sitting on.

"You can't pick someone famous and use their normal name!" Justin was practically yelling.

The others looked away, down at their laps, at their boots. But Charlene couldn't let it go.

"Why don't you just chill?" she said.

"Why don't you shut the fuck up, Charlene? Why don't you just drink some of your herbal PMS tea?"

No one said anything. Outside, they could hear male voices yelling in Arabic. The vehicle inched forward, then stopped again.

There was another long, tense silence.

"Snoop Dogg versus Flavor Flav," Mitchell said finally.

Wolf looked over at him. "Why don't you just shut up, Mitchell? Can't you tell no one feels like playing anymore?"

MATT'S THIGH MUSCLES WERE TWITCHING AS HE CLIMBED OUT of the Stryker and he wondered if it was the Stay Alert Gum. Or the second cup of instant coffee he'd had. Or both.

McNally had paired him up with Charlene again, but this time she didn't act all offended and she kept a normal pace.

"You have plenty of water in your CamelBak?" she said.

He didn't want her babying him. But he didn't want to pile on right after Justin had been so hard on her. So he just didn't say anything.

They walked along a main thoroughfare in clusters of two, simply taking in the situation. It was a commercial district and the street was lined mainly with open stalls selling spare auto parts and the Iraqi equivalent of car-repair joints. Before the cease-fire this was an iffy neighborhood; the U.S. troops suspected some of the vendors of selling IED parts to the insurgents. So the squad entered the area a little more cautiously than they had at the market.

Charlene stuck close by him this time. "What's the

matter with your pal Justin?" she said eventually.

Matt shrugged. "How would I know?"

He was sorry the minute he'd said it. Charlene was just trying to make conversation, but it annoyed him to be connected with Justin and his little temper tantrum. And it was strange the way the whole squad got quiet when Justin blew up. What was that about?

He took a sip of water, then turned to Charlene. "So how many days left in the cease-fire? You think they'll extend it?"

"I don't know, Duffy," she said. "I'm just a woman. They don't tell us anything."

She was still mad. He tried another approach. "What's the first thing you're going to do when you get back home?"

She stopped in her tracks. "You serious?" she said.

He nodded. It dawned on him that no one really talked to Charlene much. She was probably dying for someone to just shoot the shit with.

"You won't tell the guys?"

He nodded again.

"Go to a Rangers game."

Matt checked to make sure she wasn't goofing on him.

"Me and my mom," she said. "We have season tickets."

Charlene's face had softened, and for a minute Matt

entertained the possibility that she might actually be sort of good-looking. If she had on regular clothes. And makeup. And if she smiled.

Then she did smile. "Twenty-five days and counting."

"What?"

"That's right, dude. Three weeks and three days from now, I'll be on a plane home."

Matt sighed. He had more than five months left on his tour. "Does that mean you'll be sending me some Little Debbies next month?"

Charlene shrugged. "You never know."

They passed a car-repair stall where an old man was sitting on a white plastic chair, yelling at his young helper, who was lying on the ground faceup, working on the underside of a car. The old guy was angry; he was waving a wrench at the kid and shouting insults over the noise of a nearby radio.

Matt felt himself tense up. He told himself there was no threat. The guy was old. He was angry, but not at them. And all he had in his hand was a wrench. Matt took a deep breath as he walked by, but he had an uneasy feeling, a slight sense of apprehension, as he passed the man.

"Maybe I'll send you Rice Krispie Treats. . . ." Charlene was saying. "Or how 'bout some brownies. . . ."

Matt wasn't listening. He heard the static of a radio, then a few chords of a song. An Arabic love song. He spun around and aimed his weapon at the man.

The man dropped his wrench and it fell to the ground with a clank. He stood up, his hands in the air. He was terrified. In an instant, the other men on the street had gathered. They were shouting at Matt, cursing him.

Then Charlene was next to him, talking in a low, steady voice. "At ease, Duff," she said. "No hostile intent here. You hear me? No hostiles."

Matt lowered his weapon. He stood still and watched the men mouthing curses under their breath as they dispersed. But what he heard was the song. The quivering voice of a woman hung in the air.

Charlene nudged him forward and they continued walking. "What the fuck was that all about?" she said when they were a few yards away.

He didn't answer. They walked on, then he stopped and pulled out the bottle of headache pills Kwong had given him.

Charlene looked at him. Her smile was long gone; her usual disapproving expression was back.

Matt didn't care. "My fucking head is killing me."

It was near the end of their shift when Matt felt a tug on his sleeve. He spun around, his gun at the ready.

It was a little girl. A little girl with wild, tangled hair in a dirty yellow dress. She didn't say anything. She didn't even flinch at the gun barrel pointed just inches from her face. She simply looked up at him, cupped her hand, and silently put it to her open mouth, as if she were eating an imaginary heel of bread.

Matt lowered his gun and stood there looking into her mournful brown eyes. Then he shouldered his weapon, turned, and walked away.

He collapsed, fully dressed, onto his cot the minute they got back. He didn't even bother to take his boots off. He woke up, at some point later, dimly aware of the smell of food—stew—but he was too tired to eat. Later, he heard the stutter of fake, computer-generated machine-gun fire. Someone was playing Halo. He opened his eyes and saw Justin, his face lit by the bluish glow of the video game screen, then he fell back to sleep.

He woke up in the middle of the night, though, to pee. It was probably all that water Charlene had made him drink. That and the fact that he'd been asleep since four in the afternoon. He tried to go back to sleep, but every time he closed his eyes, he heard that song from the radio and it started the whole thing all over again. The alley. The candy wrapper fluttering on the razor wire, the dog trotting by.

He sat up and swung his legs over the side of the cot. Itchy gave him a dirty look as Matt dislodged him from his spot at the foot of the bed. He bent over, his head in his hands, and tried to make the replay of images stop. Tried to will himself to forget. To turn it off.

He thought about what Father Brennan had said. "Be still. And know." At the time, it had seemed profound; now it was just an empty expression. He pictured Father Brennan sitting in the linen closet, his head bowed, and finally he knew what to do.

He stood, turned to face his cot, then got down on his knees and prayed.

THEY WERE BACK PATROLLING THE AL-HIKMA MOSQUE sector again, but it was some kind of festival, some religious thing, and the streets were more crowded than usual. With women, especially, many of them in billowing black dresses—*abayas*—that covered all but their faces and hands. The women had seemed strange, otherworldly, to Matt when he first arrived in Iraq, as if they'd stepped out of a distant century and into streets full of cars and trucks and radios and cell phones.

But as time went on, he came to see past the yards and yards of black fabric and notice their faces, especially their eyes. With every other aspect of their bodies covered, their eyes took on an almost mysterious importance. Matt knew better than to stare, but he often found himself hoping to catch them in an unguarded moment—for a hint of who they really were under all that fabric.

Matt tried to gauge the mood of the crowd. The streets were lively, the air thick with the smell of cardamom, coffee, black pepper, and there was a celebratory feeling in the air. The people were almost friendly, as friendly as he'd ever seen. And he had a sudden pang of something—fondness? goodwill?—for the Iraqi people.

He wouldn't tell the guys, though. They'd make fun of him for sounding like a beauty-pageant contestant. But in that moment, he really did wish for peace. So these people could go back to living their lives. And so that he could go home. And see Caroline and his mom and Lizzy. And go to McDonald's. And drink a cold beer. He smiled at the thought that it would be a lot easier to find someone to buy him a six-pack now that he was a vet.

He'd prayed last night for some peace of mind, some grace, to help him to stop thinking about Ali and to get back to soldiering. He was no good to the squad the way he'd been acting lately and he'd asked for the willpower to go back to being the soldier he used to be, the guy who could be counted on to look out for his buddies. Maybe, he thought as he looked around at the people milling happily around him, God had answered his prayers.

He was also a little more relaxed because he hadn't had any coffee today. No Stay Alert Gum. And no headache pills, either. The coffee and the gum made him twitchy; the pills made his head fuzzy. A bad combination. He was jumpy and out of it at the same time.

Charlene was a few feet away watching a bunch of kids splash water on each other from a roadside ditch. She was actually smiling.

Matt started walking toward her. He would tell Charlene she could stop worrying about him, that he was fine now. He was. He really was.

He was heading toward her when an old man, leaning heavily on a cane, crossed his path, a pair of goats in tow. Matt stopped for a minute to let the man pass. And in that momentary pause, he heard the scratch of static, then the wail of a muezzin broadcast from high atop a minaret somewhere nearby.

The sound was like a short, sharp current of electricity coursing straight through him. All muezzin calls were slightly different. But this was the exact same one he'd heard the afternoon he was trapped in the alley.

He spun around to see where it was coming from. There was a slender white minaret just over his left shoulder. He turned again to get his bearings. About a block away, up ahead, he saw the bootleg shop where he and Justin had bought a copy of *Spider-Man 3*. He was only a block away from the alley.

The voice of the muezzin, high and quavering, echoed in the air. Matt was aware of movement around him, a vendor pulling the gate over his store, an old man rolling his prayer rug next to the stall where he sold used tires. All around him, people were preparing to pray. But it sounded as if the muezzin were calling directly to Matt.

He walked over to Charlene. "I need you to cover for me," he said.

She looked puzzled.

He shook his head. "I don't mean covering fire. I need to go somewhere right now and I need you to cover for me if anybody asks."

She held her hand up like a police officer stopping traffic. "Oh no, you don't."

"I have to, Charlene," he said. "And I'm going whether you help me or not."

She shook her head. "You and your little Rambo buddy might pull that kind of shit but not me."

"What do you mean?"

"I'm not taking off down some dead-end alley with you," she said. "I like the rules, Duffy. And I like staying alive."

Matt tried to grasp what she was saying.

"And McNally's not going to let that shit slide a second time. You guys got away with it last time because there was no officer present, but . . ." She looked behind them, down the street, where the rest of the squad was patrolling.

Matt took a step back as her words sunk in.

He and Justin were never supposed to be in that alley. To follow an insurgent vehicle down a main street was one thing, but it was suicide to chase them into the maze of dead-end streets in Baghdad where snipers would be waiting. Why hadn't that occurred to him before?

He turned away from Charlene and started walking.

She grabbed him by the sleeve. "Don't be an idiot," she said.

"I'm not asking you to come with me," he said. "Just say . . ."

"Just say it wasn't bad enough almost getting killed once? That you want to go back for seconds?"

"Say whatever you want," he said, and wrenched free of her grip.

THE OVERTURNED CAR WAS STILL THERE ON THE RIGHT-HAND side of the street. The plaster wall above it was pitted with bullet holes. That was where Matt had been pinned down.

He looked up to where the sniper had been shooting at him. That wall was also flecked with bullet holes.

And in between, on the sidewalk, there was a giant crater where the RPG had exploded.

He didn't linger there; he walked quickly up the alleyway, determined to see the spot where Ali had died, moving as fast as he could before he lost his nerve.

It was just a doorway. A set of mud-brick steps winding up to a second floor. There was no sign that anything had happened there. Matt didn't know what he expected.

Bloodstains would have been washed away long ago. He ran his hand over the steps, then along the rough, plastered wall until his fingers found it. A single bullet hole. Right behind the corner where Ali had slumped over, dead.

There it was. Proof that it had really happened, just the way he imagined it. He closed his eyes and whispered a brief prayer for forgiveness. From God. From Ali.

Then he turned and walked back down the alleyway. There was no time to be emotional. He had to get back to the squad before anyone noticed he was gone. He tried to pick up a jog, but his legs were heavy and uncooperative, and so he walked on, scanning the windows to make sure no one was watching.

No one was living on the street anymore. But there was one window that caught his eye. It was across the alley from the doorway where Ali had stood, on the second floor. A tattered gray curtain waved from behind it, and all around it, the wall was scarred with bullet holes.

The ground beneath Matt's feet seemed to tilt. He stopped and stared at the window. It had a perfect line of vision toward the doorway where Ali had been shot. The pavement seemed to heave up again, then pitch forward. He was going to pass out here in a dead-end alley—easy prey for one of the insurgents who hid in this warren of bombed-out buildings.

Matt closed his eyes. And saw the whole thing all over again. He saw Ali being lifted off his feet by the blast, saw his expression change from delight to terror.

He opened his eyes and looked back toward the doorway. The angle at which Ali's body fell meant he'd been shot from across the alley. From the window with the tattered curtain.

Where Justin had been positioned.

THE WHOLE SQUAD WAS MILLING AROUND AT THE CORNER, right in front of the bootleg store. They must have been looking for him. He swallowed and walked toward them.

"Jesus Christ!" said McNally. "A donkey cart loses a wheel and traffic is tied up for twenty minutes. Duffy, get over there with Charlene and direct cars over thataway." He pointed toward a street across the intersection.

McNally hadn't even noticed he was gone. Matt glanced over at Charlene. Her expression gave nothing away.

Matt crossed the street to join her on the other side of the intersection and started diverting the traffic—a line of beat-up cars and carts—in the other direction.

169

"Well?" Charlene said after a few minutes.

She didn't say any more than that. If she'd asked what he found, then she'd have information she might not really want. Another version of "Don't Ask, Don't Tell."

"I'm all right," he said. "I really am. You don't have to worry about me."

She considered this, then turned toward the line of cars. "I told them you had to take a leak."

It took a minute for this to sink in.

"The advantage of being paired up with a female," she said. "I couldn't exactly go with you, could I?"

Matt blinked. "Char—"

"Let's just forget about it," she said.

MATT FINISHED OUT HIS SHIFT AS TRAFFIC COP, BARELY PAYING attention to what he was doing. A kind of fog had lifted for him when he saw the alley. And he couldn't stop picturing the line of fire between the window with the curtain, where Justin had been, and the window diagonally across the street, where the sniper had been.

But he was still confused. Why had Justin fired at Ali—in the doorway on the ground floor—if the sniper was in the window on the second floor? The two positions were far apart, not even in the same line of fire. And Justin was an excellent shot, the best in the whole battalion.

It made no sense. Worse than that, it meant that Justin had shot Ali intentionally.

Matt pushed that idea out of his head. Justin could be a hot dog sometimes, a little too gung ho, but he wouldn't have killed an innocent person, a little kid, a kid he knew, no less. There was no way.

Charlene had implied that McNally had known they'd disobeyed orders going into that alley and that he "let it slide." That didn't make sense, either. McNally wouldn't sanction an unauthorized mission that had nearly gotten one of his men killed.

Now they were in the Stryker, on their way back to base, and Matt was sitting directly across from Justin. No one was in the mood for games now. They never were. The joking all took place on the way to a mission. It kept them from thinking about what you were about to face. On the way home, though, people were always exhausted. Even if it had been an uneventful patrol. It didn't matter. The sheer tension of walking a street where anything could happen, at any moment, was so grueling that if you lived through it, you just wanted to forget about it and stare into space.

WHEN THEY GOT BACK TO BASE, MCNALLY PULLED MATT aside, around the corner of the building.

"You okay, kid?"

McNally was only a couple years older than Matt—he'd dropped out of college and joined up when his parents kicked him out the house—but Matt didn't usually mind him referring to him as "kid." At the moment, though, McNally looked, not angry exactly, but not happy, either.

"Yeah, sure, Sarge," he said. "Fine."

"No bladder problems I need to know about?"

Matt gave him a puzzled look.

McNally moved his tongue around behind his lower lip, adjusting a pinch of tobacco. He spit, then looked Matt over head to toe.

"I don't know what the hell you think you were doing today, going off by yourself. . . ." He paused. "But from now on, you and Charlene are Siamese twins. Do you understand?"

Matt swallowed. "Yes, sir."

McNally stepped closer. He took hold of the straps of Matt's flak jacket, and yanked on them, just hard enough to pull Matt toward him, so close that Matt could see a tiny scar over his left eye.

"Good," he said. "Because I wouldn't want you to end up in that hospital again."

He let go, and Matt rocked back on his heels. "Yes, sir."

"Now go clean the shitters. I want you to get rid of all that graffiti."

As Matt walked away he had that uncomfortable tingling feeling on the back of his neck, as if McNally were still watching him. He went straight to the supply shed and pulled out the mop and cleaning supplies before he turned around to check. He was gone, but Matt still couldn't shake the feeling.

He didn't like being in trouble with McNally. He was a good squad leader, a guy who really cared about his troops. But it was strange that McNally hadn't actually asked Matt what he'd been doing when he wandered off. Just like Brody. He didn't want to know because then he might have to do something about it.

THE WALLS OF THE LATRINES WERE COVERED IN GRAFFITI—
most of it angry black scribbling about Osama bin Laden,
George Bush, about how hot it was in Iraq or about how
bad it smelled in the latrines. But there was also a series
of ever-escalating Chuck Norris jokes that had started
when they first set up camp.

*They once made a Chuck Norris toilet paper, but it
wouldn't take shit from anybody.*

*Chuck Norris is not hung like a horse. Horses are hung
like Chuck Norris.*

*There is no such thing as a lesbian, there are just girls
who've never met Chuck Norris.*

Matt always smiled at that last one, no matter how
many times he'd seen it.

But he wasn't smiling now as he swabbed the floor
with a mop and tried to make sense of what he'd seen
in the alley, of what Charlene had told him, and of what
McNally had said to him a few minutes ago.

At the moment he was focused on what Charlene
said about Justin playing Rambo, about pursuing the
insurgents down a dead-end alley. How had they even
ended up there, if it was against SOP?

He was down on his knees, scrubbing away at another Chuck Norris joke in black Magic Marker: *96% of all women lose their virginity to Chuck Norris. The other 4% are fat.*

The stall door swung open. It was Justin.

"Chuck Norris doesn't clean latrines," Justin said.

"Yeah, he gives them a roundhouse kick." Matt surprised himself by how easily he was able to fall back into the old routine. But at least Justin was talking to him. And they were alone. This was his chance.

"I saw you talking to McNally," Justin said.

"So?"

"So, don't fuck things up."

"What? What are you talking about?"

"Just let it go."

"Justin—"

But Justin had already left.

THEY WERE ON THEIR WAY TO PATROL THE MARKET AGAIN. It was a nice day—by Baghdad standards. Only ninety-two degrees. But Matt's every move was sluggish and his head was as cloudy as it had been that first day in the hospital. Like having a hangover, except without the good time beforehand.

The rest of the squad was in high spirits, though. At their morning briefing McNally had announced that the cease-fire had been extended. Supposedly, there were even talks with the Iraqi government about a date for U.S. troops to go home. No one wanted to jinx it, though, so instead of talking about the cease-fire, the other guys were playing the Game.

"Madonna versus Pink." Figueroa had a thing for Madonna. He was always throwing her name out.

"Dude, we're sick of Madonna," Wolf said. "You just used her last week against Larry King."

"So what? She beat him."

Matt popped a piece of Stay Alert Gum in his mouth as he climbed out of the vehicle. He jogged a few steps to loosen up, aware that his leg was dragging again.

They fanned out in pairs, the way they had every day this week. Wolf and Figueroa went first, then Justin and Mitchell, Matt and Charlene last. Matt took a sip of water from his CamelBak and followed along behind Charlene. McNally stayed with the vehicle to monitor the radio.

"You look like shit," Charlene said.

Matt managed a wan smile. "You know I'm not just eye candy, right?"

Charlene frowned. "And what's with your leg? You limping?"

He didn't say anything, but he made a note to himself to be sure to walk behind Charlene today so she wouldn't be able to keep a close eye on him.

As if she could read his mind, she turned around and walked on, keeping a slower pace than usual.

The mood in the market was lively, like it was the day of the festival. People took their time shopping, milling around the various stalls, stopping to watch an old man dancing in front of a boom box instead of scurrying from stall to stall as they had before the ceasefire. And a guy who ran a tea shop offered the whole squad free cups of chai.

"Peace! Peace!" the man said through his missing teeth as he pushed the chai on them.

Even Charlene seemed to get into the spirit. Matt was leaning against a post watching as she tried to communicate with a man selling rugs.

"Beautiful," she said as the man held up one small prayer rug after another.

Matt could tell—from the polite smile frozen on her face—that Charlene was just trying to be friendly. But he also knew that the man was hoping to make a sale. After Charlene had looked at all the rugs without making an offer, the man snapped his fingers and gestured to his son to get more samples from the back of the stall.

Charlene shook her head. "Beautiful," she shouted, as

if that would help. "But no, thank you."

The man looked confused, then went back to the first pile of rugs. Charlene turned around and waved to Matt. "Duffy," she shouted out over the din of voices and the squawking of chickens underfoot. "Help me out here."

The sounds of the bazaar seemed to fade out as if someone had slowly turned the volume down on the TV, and Matt felt a painful pressure in his ears. There was a bright flash of light. Then a piece of metal—it looked strangely like a frying pan—flew through the air and hit Charlene in the chin. Matt watched her head snap back. Then she disappeared behind a cloud of dust.

MATT HAD BEEN THROWN TO THE GROUND BY THE FORCE OF the blast and he lay facedown in the dirt, gasping for air. He could feel heat on his cheek and registered that something was on fire nearby, but all he could see was a wall of swirling dust and sand. He scrambled to his feet and ran through the smoke toward where Charlene had been standing.

There was nothing left of the rug seller's stand except a piece of torn plastic sheeting flapping in the wind, but there was Charlene, lying on one of the rugs she'd been admiring, as if she'd decided to take a nap on it. Her eyes were open and she was staring up at the sky, a blank look on her face. Matt knelt down, grabbed her hand, and started talking to her. "You're okay," he said. "You're going to be fine."

Matt felt for her pulse. Nothing. He held his hand near her mouth, checking for breath. Nothing. Then he leaned his head against her chest to listen for a heartbeat.

Her body was soft. That was all he could think. That Charlene, the little toughy who bragged about bench-pressing more than the guys, was actually soft and girly. He put his arms around her, pulled her toward him, and rocked her back and forth in his arms.

All around him people were screaming. Things were burning. A fine gray ash was falling, like snow. While Matt burrowed his face into her shoulder and wept.

A MINUTE OR TWO LATER, HE BECAME AWARE OF GUNFIRE, NOT far away. His training took over then as he realized that a secondary attack was underway. Whoever had set off the bomb was taking advantage of the chaos to fire at the Americans who'd survived. He laid Charlene gently on the rug and turned in the direction of the gunfire.

The explosion had gone off in the middle of a shopping district and there were buildings all around, so it took Matt a minute to figure out what was going on.

On the left side of the street he saw a line of smoke and flame. The insurgents had poured oil in a drainage ditch, then set it on fire. They were firing from behind the smoke, making it impossible for them to be seen.

On the other side of the street, behind a line of parked cars, Matt saw the tip of McNally's long radio antenna quivering in the air. He couldn't see the guys in his squad, but he saw muzzle flashes as they fired in the direction of the flaming ditch.

From the angle where he was, Matt could only see the exchange of fire; he couldn't really see the men on either side.

Then the wind shifted for a moment and he saw, from behind the smoking ditch, an enemy fighter—a young bearded guy in a blue track suit—hoisting a grenade launcher on his shoulder. He struggled under the weight of the weapon for a moment, then dropped back down behind the smoke screen.

Matt propped his M16 on the hood of a nearby car and adjusted the scope. The scene was blurry at first, nothing but flames and debris.

Then, with one fractional turn on the scope, the guy

in the track suit popped into focus. It was a strangely intimate feeling, the way the high-powered lens brought him so close.

Matt placed his finger on the trigger. But he couldn't steady it, couldn't make it bend, couldn't make it stop shaking.

He took his eye away from the lens and saw Justin leaning out from behind a car, getting ready to make a run in the direction of McNally's antenna. He had a weird look on his face, like he was lost or something.

Matt looked through the scope again. The guy in the track suit was aiming the grenade launcher at Justin. Matt held his breath and tapped his finger against the trigger.

It was as if the bullet left his weapon in slow motion. Matt could see it boring through the air in front of him, traveling inch by inch by inch past the buildings in the alley, until finally it disappeared into the flames.

THE FIRING STOPPED. THERE WAS A LONG, EERIE SILENCE. MATT counted to one hundred. Then to one hundred again. He picked up Charlene's body and started to walk in the direction of McNally's antenna. But a few seconds after he stepped out into the open, he heard the *ching, ching, ching* of rounds going by overhead. He ducked behind a flimsy wooden market table that must have been blown into the street by the explosion. He peered around the side of the table and saw Justin crouched behind one of the cars, gesturing to him.

"C'mon!" he yelled. "Get over here."

But Matt couldn't move.

Then Justin stepped out from behind the car and started firing, giving cover so Matt would have time to make a run for it. That somehow brought Matt back to his senses. He pulled Charlene's body close and tried to run. His right leg trembled under the weight, but somehow he made it to the other side of the street just as a bullet *pinged* against the hood of the car.

Figueroa took Charlene from him and laid her gently on a tarp that had been spread out on the ground behind them. There was another American soldier lying on the tarp, facedown. Parts of his uniform were burned off— but not the small wolf decal on the back of his helmet. Wolf.

Matt slumped down, his back against the car, and a minute later he felt Justin sit down next to him, cursing under his breath.

The firing had stopped. There was an uneasy quiet. Then a deafening roar as a U.S. helicopter came out of nowhere. A barrage of missiles rained on the building behind the ditch. The structure crumbled like a sand castle, and the chopper flew off.

It took Matt a couple minutes to understand that the blood on his hands and all over the front of his uniform was Charlene's. And a few more minutes to realize that the pool of blood on the ground next to him was Justin's.

Mitchell and Figueroa and McNally were staring in awe at the wreckage of the building across the street. But Matt was still sitting on the ground looking at his hands. And Justin was sitting next to him and cursing and pawing at his leg, like he was trying to get something out of his pocket.

Matt turned and looked over at Justin. There was a rip in his pants—and a puddle of blood on the ground beneath his leg.

Matt got to his knees, put his hand over Justin's wound, and yelled for a medic. When the other guys realized what was going on, McNally got on the radio and started shouting for a medic. And Mitchell and Figueroa ran off to get help.

Matt had positioned himself so he was straddling Justin as he sat propped up against the car. He was leaning forward, both hands on the wound, face-to-face with him as he pressed down to stop the bleeding.

Justin winced, then gritted his teeth.

"It's okay, man," Matt said. "Medic's on his way."

"Dude," Justin said, "I . . ."

"Just take it easy, dude," Matt said. "Don't try to talk."

Justin shook his head. "I did it, you know," he said.

Matt knew exactly what "it" was. "Let's talk about that later, dude," Matt said. "Like when you take me fishing at that place near your house."

Beads of sweat were running down Justin's face and he was breathing fast, but he acted like he hadn't heard. "It was my fault we were in that alley in the first place. It was my fault you got pinned down behind that car."

Matt shook his head. "Shut up, man. Forget about it."

Matt looked over his shoulder. McNally was shouting into the radio, trying to describe their location. Where the hell was the medic? Where the hell were Mitchell and Figueroa?

"He wasn't who you thought he was," Justin said. "Ali."

"What do you mean?"

Matt looked in Justin's eyes. His pupils were like

184

black pinpricks. A sign of shock, maybe. Maybe that's why he was going on about Ali. Or maybe he needed to get it off his chest. Either way, Matt didn't want to hear what he was saying.

"Take it easy," Matt said. "Just stop talking, okay?"

Justin shook his head. "What do you think he was doing in that alley?"

Matt looked away, at his fingers, at the blood seeping out between them.

"He was a spotter, Matt. He was relaying information about your position so they could adjust their fire."

Everything stopped. The sirens. The crackling of the burning building across the street. McNally cursing into the radio.

Then everything seemed to happen very quickly. A medic was kneeling down next to Matt. He removed Matt's hands from the wound and started cutting Justin's pant leg open with scissors. Another medic shouldered his way in between Matt and Justin and started an IV in Justin's arm. Matt rocked back on his heels and stared at Justin through the crowd that had seemed to gather around him. Mitchell and Figueroa were back. McNally was there. Everyone was talking at once.

Then Justin was being lifted onto a stretcher. He was cursing and being carried away as Matt knelt on the ground, watching pairs of khaki legs shuffle past him.

The next thing Matt heard was gravel spraying as the ambulance pulled away.

MATT WAS IN SOME KIND OF ABANDONED WAREHOUSE, sitting on the floor, his helmet in his lap. A medic had just come by to check him over, then left, telling him to eat something. "Have a drink of water," he said. "Relax."

It was a stupid thing to say. Two of his squad members were dead. Justin was injured. And he was supposed to relax.

But people were saying all kinds of weird things. Mitchell had said something about Wolf's little sister sending him Rice Krispie Treats. He was in shock, apparently, curled up on the floor next to Matt in a fetal position, an army blanket around his shoulders. And McNally was in a corner, punching his fist into his thigh, muttering.

Matt had heard of guys saying crazy things when they were injured; he'd heard of a guy asking about what would happen to his motorcycle if he died. Mainly they called out for their mothers.

But Justin had been pretty coherent. He'd said it was

his fault they were in the alley. That it was his fault Matt had gotten pinned down.

Matt thought back to the moment they'd jumped out of the Humvee to chase the guys who ran the roadblock. He pictured Justin running across the alley, his head down. Justin had been so intent on catching them, so intent on being the hero, that he hadn't stopped to realize what a dangerous situation he'd gotten into.

It *was* Justin's fault that they'd been in the alley. But that didn't mean the rest of it was true. That Ali was a spy.

Ali was just a kid. A pest. A tagalong who was always following them around.

Justin had made up the part about Ali being an enemy sympathizer to cover up for what he'd done. To get his Bronze Star.

Matt leaned his head against the wall and closed his eyes. And he saw the whole thing all over again. The alley. The candy wrapper fluttering on the razor wire. The dog trotting by. Sparks on the pavement. Ali being lifted off his feet, smiling and slowly paddling his arms like a swimmer, floating into the air until finally all Matt could see were the soles of his shoes.

Matt sat up straight and opened his eyes. The boy floating through the air had been wearing shoes. Soccer cleats.

There was only one way a street kid like Ali could

have gotten a pair of shoes, especially soccer cleats. From the insurgents.

A SHORT, STOCKY GUY, A MIDDLE-AGED SOLDIER WITH SQUARE black glasses, showed up at the barracks when they got back that night. "I'm sorry," he said. "But I wonder if any of you fellas can help me with the personal effects."

Figueroa had been writing to his wife. Mitchell was in bed, asleep, still dressed. And Matt had been sitting on the edge of his cot, his head in his hands. Thinking. And thinking and thinking.

"Personal effects," the guy repeated. "Any belongings we might send home to their loved ones."

Figueroa shook his head and looked at Matt. His chin was quivering. "I can't do it, man."

And so Matt got up and walked over to Wolf's cot, carefully taking the picture of his dog that he'd taped on the wall behind his bed, the thong they'd used for capture the flag, and a letter from his kid sister. The letter, in careful elementary school penmanship, started off *Dear Meathead*.

Matt went through the motions of packing up all of Wolf's stuff as if he were observing the process from a distance. As he folded one of Wolf's shirts, he watched his hands smooth the fabric, making precise military folds, and noted with detachment that he was touching something that Wolf had worn just yesterday, something that now belonged to a dead man. The guy with the square glasses stood next to him with a clipboard, making a list of everything like he was taking inventory.

When they'd packed everything into three hard plastic black boxes and sealed them with duct tape, Matt helped him load them onto a Humvee.

Matt stopped when he saw two other boxes and a guitar case on the back of the Humvee. A tag on the handle of the guitar case said, *Charlene Hughes, KIA. 31 Fairview Road, Black Springs, PA.*

In a few hours, Charlene's mother would open the front door and see an army chaplain on her porch. Right now, though, she was sleeping or maybe watching TV. Her daughter was dead. She just didn't know it yet.

A female officer was in the front seat of the Humvee holding a clipboard. It registered with Matt that she had gone to Charlene's bunk and packed up her stuff. The guy with the square glasses clapped Matt on the shoulder. "I'm sorry, son," he said. "I really am." Then he got into the front seat and started the engine.

Matt stared at the boxes that held the last possessions of his friends. Stupid stuff, like the Christmas lights

Wolf had strung around his bed, Charlene's stuffed animal. Without even realizing it, Matt had grabbed hold of the fender. The car shifted into drive, but Matt was still hanging on. The vehicle suddenly rocked forward, and Matt watched as his hands turned white, then let go, as he fell on his butt and watched the Humvee pull away. He sat there, on the ground, sobbing, until long after the taillights disappeared.

HE WASN'T WHO YOU THOUGHT HE WAS, JUSTIN HAD SAID.

He was just a kid, Matt had kept telling himself. And it was true. A kid who liked Skittles and American slang. A kid who could score a goal from twenty yards out, barefoot.

He was also an orphan who lived in a drainage pipe, a kid who was so hungry, so desperate, he'd do anything.

He *was* a kid—until someone gave him a pair of soccer cleats. After that, he was an enemy sympathizer. A spy. A spotter who had nearly gotten Matt killed.

And Matt was a fool. He'd thought he was a good guy, the kind of guy who handed out art supplies to little kids and played soccer with them. But it was his friendship with Ali that had gotten the boy killed. He'd thought it was Justin who'd put them in danger. But by befriending Ali, Matt had actually put the whole squad at risk.

Figueroa came over to bum a smoke. "Do you think we should be worried about Mitchell?" he said. "He hasn't moved in, like, hours."

Matt shrugged. "I don't know. I know when you have a concussion they wake you up every hour so you don't go into a coma or something."

They just stared at Mitchell's big, hulking form under the blanket. Itchy was curled up at the foot of the bed.

"So tell me, did everyone know?" Matt said.

"About what?"

"About what happened the day I got hurt."

Figueroa took a long pull on his cigarette. "We knew something went down. But we didn't know what, exactly." He shrugged, "Justin got kinda weird after that—snapping at people, trying to get out of patrol duty. McNally was going to send him to a headshrinker."

"What do you mean?"

Figueroa took another long drag on his cigarette, exhaled, then studied the smoke pouring out of his nostrils. "He wouldn't want anyone to know this, okay?"

Matt waited.

"Justin couldn't pull the trigger after that."

The words hit Matt like a body blow.

Figueroa examined his cigarette. It had burned down so low, he didn't even take another drag. He stamped it out underfoot.

"You won't tell anyone?" he said.

Matt could barely nod.

"Well, today, when that bomb blew up, he freaked. When Wolf got hit, Justin lost it. Went running for McNally, like, I don't know, like a baby running to its mother."

Matt remembered the strange look on Justin's face: he had been terrified.

"Then, all of a sudden, a couple minutes later, he jumps out from behind the car and starts shooting. Instant Rambo." Figueroa headed back to his bed. "Go figure."

Matt sank down onto his cot. What happened in the alley that day had haunted them both—had shaken them up so much that they'd nearly stopped being soldiers. But when it had mattered most, Justin still had his back and he had Justin's.

THE NEXT DAY WAS RIDICULOUSLY BEAUTIFUL. A RARE Baghdad day when there was a slight breeze in the air. The leaves of the palm trees were whispering and the air smelled like fresh-baked bread and cardamom. Even the sun seemed benign.

McNally was outside in what used to be the school play yard. He had set up a rifle leaning against a pair of boots, and he was about to put the helmet on top of the rifle butt. The traditional setup for a memorial service in the field. Something Matt hadn't seen since Benson was killed. Something he didn't want to see.

He was about to leave when McNally looked up at him. His eyes were red and swollen and he looked like hell.

Matt didn't say anything, he just knelt down next to McNally and helped him set up the second rifle and pair of boots. One for Wolf. One for Charlene.

"I'm sorry," McNally whispered. Matt couldn't tell if McNally was talking to him or to the memorial he'd set up. "I let you down."

Matt didn't know what to say.

"I saw this guy with a green backpack," McNally said,

turning to face Matt. "Near the chai seller. He looked me right in the eye. Walked up to Wolf and asked for a smoke. Then he did it. Pulled the strap. Blew himself sky high. Wolf never even had a chance."

Matt wanted to yell and curse and punch someone. But he was too sad, and too exhausted, to do anything but sit there.

McNally shook his head. "These people . . ."

Matt thought about what Charlene had said when Ali stole his sunglasses. *That's what happens when you try to make friends with these people.* And he thought about what Wolf had said about being in Iraq. *We came over here to help these people and instead we're killing them.*

They were both right.

Matt helped McNally to his feet, then took hold of the straps on his vest, just the way McNally had done the day he made Matt clean the latrines. "Sarge," he said, "it wasn't your fault."

McNally gripped the straps on Matt's vest and looked him in the eye. "And Duffy." His voice was firm, as if he were giving an order. "What happened in the alley, that wasn't your fault, either."

THEIR SQUAD—WHAT WAS LEFT OF IT—WAS ON REST AND recovery that day because of what had happened to them in the market. Sometime around lunchtime, Mitchell had gotten up to pee, then went straight back to sleep. Figueroa was reading *Let God Handle It* and writing down what he would say at the memorial service later on. And Matt was staring at the bare wall where Wolf's mementos had been when McNally walked in. He was holding a yellow form of some kind, about to give an order, but he stopped at the doorway at the sight of the empty beds.

Matt got up, went over to him, and gestured to the form. "What's this, Sarge?"

McNally shook his head slightly, as if he were waking up. "I, uh, I have to go on a supply run," he said. "Anyone want to go with me?"

Matt grabbed his helmet and stood up. Anything was better than sitting around the barracks and thinking.

McNALLY DROVE THE HUMVEE AS MATT STARED OUT THE window. They weren't going far, only to a makeshift warehouse where the army stored spare tires, extra sleeping bags, that sort of thing. They weren't even going outside the wire, the area of the town that the army had secured months ago and cordoned off with concrete blast walls and razor wire.

It was one of the more peaceful parts of town. There were a handful of restaurants where the men sat at outdoor tables, sipping tea and reading newspapers. The women milled around in the market, gossiping and squeezing the produce. And the children went to school carrying backpacks decorated with American cartoon characters. There was even an ice-cream vendor.

But all Matt saw as they drove along were threats. Every tea seller was an enemy soldier. Every woman was a spy. Every backpack held a bomb.

McNally pulled up in front of the warehouse and cut the engine. "You coming?" he said.

Matt shook his head. "I'll wait out here."

He got out, slung his weapon over his shoulder, and leaned against the back of the Humvee. A good place to keep an eye on anyone who went past.

It was a quiet morning, but Matt noticed an Iraqi man with a big belly strolling by on the other side of the street, talking on a cell phone. Slowly, Matt's finger sought out the trigger pad of the rifle at his side. He squinted at the man, keeping him in view until he turned down a side street. A few minutes later, a gang of young men came by, guys Matt's own age, wearing Western shirts and sweaters, carrying books. They were arguing in lively, animated voices, jabbing one another now and then to make a point. Matt straightened up, planted his boots on the ground, and glowered at them. One of the boys spotted him and pointed to the others. Their voices fell silent as they scurried past.

Then the door to the school across the street flew open with a *clang*. Little girls in blue jumpers and crisp white blouses and little boys in navy trousers and white shirts came spilling out into a dusty lot ringed by a tall fence. The everyday sounds of the street faded and the air was filled with the sounds of shrieking and laughing as the kids raced around the lot playing.

Matt pulled a cigarette out of his pack and tried to light it, but it didn't catch. He tried again with no luck, then tossed the cigarette into the gutter and grabbed another one. His head was bowed, his hand cupped over the flame, when he heard it. The soft *pock* of someone kicking a soccer ball. He looked up and saw the black-and-white ball as it flew over the fence and bounced into the middle of the road.

He inhaled and narrowed his gaze. Coming down the road, a few hundred yards away, was a bus.

A few of the kids ran to the fence and shouted at him. They pointed to the ball and jumped up and down.

But Matt couldn't seem to move. The ball had rolled to a stop. And the bus was getting closer. And all he could do was watch the scene unfold as if it were one of Meaghan Finnerty's test questions: If the bus is going thirty miles an hour, how long will it take to reach the soccer ball?

The teacher came to the fence and yelled angrily at him. The bus driver honked his horn. And all the kids in the yard gathered at the fence, screaming and pointing frantically.

All except one. She was smaller than the others and she'd had to crawl under their legs to get to the fence to see what was going on. Her dark hair hung down in two little braids tied with yellow ribbons.

While all the others were shrieking at him, she'd stuck her arm through the fence to give him the thumbs-up.

When the other kids looked at him, they saw just another American soldier. But the little girl with the yellow ribbons in her hair seemed to be saying I see *you*.

And so Matt dashed into the street, gave the ball a gentle kick, and watched as it sailed into the crayon-blue sky.

Acknowledgments

My deepest thanks go to the families of Army Sergeant Sherwood Baker, Army Specialist Joshua Justice Henry, Marine Lance Corporal Patrick B. Kenny, Army First Lieutenant Neil Anthony Santoriello, and Marine Lance Corporal William Brett Wightman. These families were generous, kind, and brave in sharing the stories of their sons and brothers with me. The shape of this story changed many times since we sat in their living rooms, looking at scrapbooks and revisiting cherished and sometimes painful memories, but it was in their honor that this book was written.

I would also like to thank Gunnery Sergeant Armando Felciano, Headquarters and Support Company, First Battalion, 25th Marines, for the diligence and attention to detail he brought to this book. He checked and challenged the facts in the story so that the book would be a faithful rendering of life in Iraq.

I would also like to thank Gene McMahon and the volunteers at Vets Journey Home, for allowing me to staff a remarkable workshop that helps returning vets vanquish the ghosts of combat; the American Friends Service Committee, whose exhibit "Eyes Wide Open" moved me to investigate the civilian casualties in the war in Iraq; Veterans Against the War, a group of brave and dedicated soldiers who let me camp out with them on their march to New Orleans; and the staff at the McClellan Memorial Veterans Hospital in Little Rock, Arkansas, for their patience in educating me about post-traumatic stress and traumatic brain injury.

My editor, Alessandra Balzer, once again guided me through tough terrain with intelligence, care, and poise, and my writers group, Mark Millhone and Andrea Chapin, supported and inspired me every step of the way.

Lastly, thanks to my family, who makes it possible for me to do the work I love.